W9-DIG-347

INDIGO HAZE

THUG LOVE IS THE BEST LOVE 4

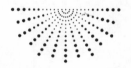

AUBREÉ PYNN

B. LOVE PUBLICATIONS

B. LOVE PUBLICATIONS

Visit bit.ly/readBLP to join our mailing list!

B. Love Publications - where Authors celebrate black men, black women, and black love.

To submit a manuscript for consideration, email your first three chapters to blovepublications@gmail.com with SUBMISSION as the subject.

Let's connect on social media!

Facebook - B. Love Publications
Twitter - @blovepub
Instagram - @blovepublications

Bit.ly/BLPWW19

NOVEMBER 2ND-3RD, 2019

BOOKS & BRUNCH
BOOK BASH & SIGNING

"Games,Raffles,
Giveaways,Music,Dancing,
Selfies,Memories, Fun!"

MEMPHIS, TN

B.LOVE PUBLICATIONS

WINTER
WONDERLAND
MEET & GREET

NOVEMBER 2ND-3RD, 2019

FEATURED AUTHORS

B. LOVE
A. JONES
SHA JUANA MCDUFFY
MONICA WALTERS
DE'SHON DREAMZ
LB'N.C
IVY LAIKA
ASHLEY
A. BRYANT
AUBREE PYNN
S.REVER
MYCAH EDWARDS
INDIA T. NORFLEET
JESS WORDS
C. MONET
COURTNEY IRVING
M.T. DIXON

A. MARIE JOHNSON
ANNITIA L. JACKSON
BRITTANI SMITH
BRITT JONI
CHE'RIDA FRANKLIN
DANIELLE ALLEN "HONORARY"
IESHA BREE
LAKISHA JOHNSON
PHYLLIS BOURNE "HONORARY"
SHANTAE
SIDAI B
NICOLE FALLS
STEPHANIE NICOLE NORRIS
KL HALL
CHRISTINA C. JONES
ALEXANDRIA HOUSE
JESSICA N. WATKINS

MEMPHIS, TN

B.LOVE PUBLICATIONS

WINTER
WONDERLAND
MEET & GREET

INTRODUCTION

To the reader:

For everyone who has stuck with this series from the beginning, I thank you for entrusting me with your vast emotions.
This series took everything out of me, so I know it took a lot out
of you. When you flip the page, the journey begins. Please
enjoy it. I cannot wait to read your reviews.

Xo,

- *A.P.*

MY JOB IS TO MAKE YOU
COMFORTABLE ENOUGH TO BE
YOURSELF...

NIPSEY HUSSLE: I DON'T STRESS

I remember feeling like a stepchild, nigga
I would hate to see my momma stressed out, nigga
I could die today I've made the set proud, nigga
And I could fly away, but I respect vows, nigga

CHAPTER ONE

*I*ndigo Sims

"I'm not telling you goofy niggas shit." Indie scoffed with laughter. "Try again, cuh."

He sat in the steel chair, halfway slouched down with his top lip curled upward. The detest was etched into the crevices of his face. Indie looked nonchalantly at the pictures of him and TK spread across the steel table. His eyes traced over the photos of Indie and TK exchanging at the party TK threw for him months ago. His eyes went from the photos back then at the detectives who sat across the table from him.

Their faces were laced with satisfaction thinking that they finally had him. Indie had been a ghost to everyone. Even when niggas were paid to get rid of him, they couldn't. He'd become an urban legend. If they couldn't get him before he sure as hell wasn't about to let them get him now.

Unwilling to tell either of the detective's shit, Indie was completely amused by their persistence. The fact that they got him down here without a fight was a miracle enough, now they were just reaching and trying their luck. He knew that eventually they were coming to talk to him so he didn't put up a fight. He also didn't need Taj upset if this happened anywhere else with him. But he'd be damned if they were going to catch him saying anything regarding TK and without Bobby present. He was actually going to sit there with a stoic expression on his face until Bobby showed up or until they got sick of asking him questions and hitting a brick wall.

"Indie, we know, that you two were involved. You've been seen with him on more than one occasion. Just tell us what we need to know. Where is he?" the older detective asked looking at Indie.

He chuckled lightly and clasped his hands together. Indie shrugged his shoulders, then ran his hand over his head. The thought of Taj pacing the floor waiting for him to come back home made him groan with irritation. "We done here? I got shit to do."

The younger detective chuckled, pulled up a seat beside Indie and sat down. "Let me just talk to you, homie. Let's get to the bottom of this and we can all go home. Okay?"

Indie cut his eye, pursed his lips, and moved his seat over. "My nigga, you don't even have to be that close to me. That's not how I get down...aight, *homie?*"

"Indigo, cut the shit, okay? Where is TK? Someone knows something. We started with you out of respect. We heard that's something you're big on...respect. You're the top guy in the streets now but you got your homeboy running your product while you sit back in that big house and chill. We will turn our eyes to your little business. Where is TK? Don't the set want to know?"

"Nigga." Indie released with a scoff that was followed by a hearty laugh. "You two trippin'. Stop with the bullshit."

Indie's eyes narrowed as they threw another picture of Ricky and Manny making a transaction. This was clearly after he told them to shut everything down. Holding his face neutral, he nodded slowly. Just as he was about to tell both of them to fuck themselves, Bobby walked in with a scowl on his face.

"Detectives...I know you didn't go to my client's home, pick him up, and bring him down here without letting him call me, especially without a warrant or a real reason behind all of this." Bobby's voice rumbled through the room as the door slammed behind him.

"He's free to go."

"Really, but yet, you're here questioning him," Bobby countered with a raised eyebrow. "This is over. Next time you want to talk to my client, do it the right way."

"Well, I guess we're done here, fellas." Indie's face formed a smirk as he rose to his feet and walked out the room. Once he was out of the precinct he looked over at Bobby and asked, "What?"

"What did you tell them?" Bobby questioned. Indie towered over him and examined the crease between Bobby's eyebrows. His expression mirrored Bobby's. "You didn't say nothing?"

"You know me. I'm a street nigga. We don't talk to them about nothing. The only reason I willingly came down to this bitch was because I didn't want them to pop off with my girl and my brother at the house. Joey can't be around none of that shit." He huffed and walked away from Bobby.

Bobby wasn't going to let it go so easily. Indie was clearly irritated but Bobby needed to make sure that Indie didn't give away any information that was going to have him sitting behind bars. "Indie, we aren't done talking."

"I am, I got shit to handle," Indie shouted over his shoulder. He made his way to Bobby's car and waited for him to pop the locks. Bobby groaned heavily and rubbed his temples. "And you're going to take me to South Central."

"Come on, Indie." Bobby shook his head unlocking his car and Indie hopped in. "Let me take you home."

"You're scared of the hood? Come on, Bobby, you represent hood niggas. So let's go ride through the hood. You don't have to stay. I just need to holla at Ricky."

Bobby hesitated before climbing inside of his 600 Benz and Indie followed suit. Pulling his phone out of his pocket, Indie hit Ricky's name and waited for him to pick up. "Yo, what's up, nigga?"

Indie grunted hearing Ricky's voice in his attempt to remain cool and level headed. But it wasn't working. He was trying his best not to explode over the phone. "Ain't shit nigga, where you at?"

"The damn buildings watching these niggas clean up and move on to the next thing," Ricky responded through the phone as Indie nodded his head like he could see him.

"Aight, bet. Stay there. I'm on my way," Indie finalized, hanging up the phone and shooting Taj a quick text.

I'm cool be back in a few.

Bobby pulled up to the commercial buildings and looked over at Indie with a pleasantly surprised expression on his face. "What's going on here?"

Indie swung the door open, climbed out of the car, and looked around. He waited for Bobby to do the same. After Bobby got out, Indie started pointing to the various buildings around them. "We have some office buildings, a few storefronts, and up the street is going to be a STEM center we're gutting out and redoing. The kids around here don't have shit to keep them off the streets."

Bobby placed his hands on his hips and whistled. "Wow. Indie...I'm proud of you."

"It ain't shit," Indie responded reaching out to shake Bobby's hand. "Thank you."

"As you say, it ain't shit. I'll be in touch," Bobby assured getting one last look around before he climbed back inside of his car. Once Bobby pulled out the parking lot, Indie made his way across to find Ricky.

Finding him in the back room they used to look over the plans for the buildings, Indie stepped further into the room and leaned on the wall with his arms crossed over his body. Ricky was smirking down at his phone before Indie cleared his throat to get his attention.

"What's good, nigga," Ricky spoke, looking Indie over. "Where you coming from?"

Indie chuckled lowly and looked down the hall at the guys working. Regardless of how bad Ricky had him fucked up, Indie respected him enough to not cause a scene.

"Ay!" Indie shouted down the hall. "Y'all go ahead and go home for the day."

Without question, the contractors packed their things and left the building leaving Ricky and Indie alone to have the conversation that was burning Indie's throat. Focusing back on Ricky, Indie hummed before pressing his temples with his thumbs. "I was down at the precinct."

"Joey home?" Ricky questioned with a smile. Indie nodded his head. "So, you went down there like that?"

"Nah, those fucks came and got me from my spot and you wouldn't guess what they wanted to talk to me about...TK. You know the typical shit. The nigga went missing and they want to know if I know anything. But the shit that's fucking me up is the pictures of you and Manny making transactions well after I told both of you simple ass niggas to stop. What part of that shit was unclear..." Indie trailed off waiting for Ricky to speak up. But the moment was short lived. "Don't make have to go ask that nigga what the fuck y'all got going on. I'm coming to you out of respect."

Ricky chuckled, placed his phone down, and flicked the tip of his nose before he looked Indie in the eyes. Indie couldn't figure out what was pissing him off more, the cockiness that oozed from Ricky's pours or his inability to express how this was an issue. "How do you think I've been funding all this?"

Indie pushed his brows together and looked his best friend up and down. "Save that bullshit for a dumb nigga. I don't need shit to fund nothing. You think I put all my cash in the bank? You crazy as fuck."

Indie was visibly pissed off. His face was red and teeth were gritted so tight Ricky could see the indentation in his jaw line. "The problem is you don't respect the game, nigga. You think you above this shit and can do whatever you want to do. I had the intention of coming over here to fuck you up but I'm not about to do that shit. You're going to have to eat the shit you serve. If you still want to be a street nigga, go do it. Separate yourself from me and all my shit because I ain't doing this. I told you when I was done that I was done."

Indie dropped his arms to his side, pushed himself off the wall and headed down the hall. He pulled his phone out of his pocket and got an Uber. Indie couldn't bring himself to put his hands on Ricky. That wasn't going to teach him shit. Ricky had to learn for himself and it wasn't a lesson that Indie could try and teach him anymore.

Standing on the curb waiting for his Uber to pull up, Indie heard Ricky's voice travel over his shoulder. Groaning a bit, Indie looked over his shoulder and watched Ricky get closer. "Yeah."

"Fuck you doing talking to the cops?" Ricky questioned as though he had ground to stand on.

"Look, bro. You don't have shit to talk to me about. Let's be real. You don't have shit to say to me but I was wrong nigga. Other than that, we don't have shit to talk about. I'm not about to be getting dragged in and out of police stations to answer to the shit you did and I would never expect you to do shit like that. Everything you do on some sneaky shit you got to answer for. I'm willing to answer to everything, including pulling that trigger. Can you say the same? I'm looking at you real funny right now. Trying to figure out where the fuck your code at, I don't see that shit. You come find me when you want to get back on the right side of this shit. Until then, Joey will be seeing about all of this."

Indie's Uber pulled up to the curb and he walked away to get in without another word. More than anything, Indie was hurt that Ricky didn't trust him enough to know that they were going to triple their money soon. But Ricky was a grown ass man and he had to be responsible for his own actions.

CHAPTER TWO

*T*aj
Her nerves were through the roof. Taj couldn't
even enjoy the beauty of Indie's beachfront home. Instead of
roaming around and taking in the scenery of waves crashing
against the ocean and the breeze coming through the cracked
window, she gnawed at the corner of her mouth. She sat on the
steps of the house anxiously biting her lip and waiting for Indie
to walk into the house. The thought of anything happening to
take him off his path was upsetting her. That was followed by
the thought of anyone taking him away from her. That unsettled her more.

"Baby," Joey spoke up walking outside and sitting on the
step by her. She flashed a small smile at him and straightened
herself up. "You good?"

Taj let a huff of air push through her nostrils and pushed
her curls out her face after letting her lip free. "No, but when he
gets here, I will be though."

Joey couldn't fight the smile that took over his face. Seeing
that after all this time Taj was still captivated by his brother

and nothing could really pull her away from him was beautiful.

"You know, growing up in the hood, you don't see shit like this," Joey stated handing her a glass of water. "Don't see shit like this. This love y'all got it's fucking beautiful although it could've been the love we shared...but I get it."

Joey's statement made Taj giggle and pull herself out of her anxiety and sigh causing her thoughts to reset. "Joey..."

"No need to let me down easy. Like I said, I get it. You're good for him. For a very long time I've watched him live for the people. He has that pioneer spirit; he wants to take everyone out their situation and make life easier for them and for a long time he lost himself because he lost you. He might never say it out of his mouth but that shit fucked with him. I'm happy he got you back, happy you let him back in." Joey's smile was wide and warm. He wrapped his arms around her and kissed her cheek. Letting her go and seeing Indie pull up in an Uber, he let out a sigh of relief. "But if he ever leaves you again...big daddy got you."

Taj burst into a fit of giggles before she stood to her feet and met Indie halfway down the sidewalk. She examined the scowl across his face and placed her hand on his chest. Indie's heart raged against his chest but the touch of Taj's hand calmed it down momentarily. Her eyes were soft and his shoulders fell slightly.

"I'm not talking about it out here," Indie rumbled. "Let's go inside."

She nodded her head and walked inside the house in front of him. Joey closed the door behind them and looked at Indie run his hand over his face with agitation. "Joey, I'm going to need you to go to the site tomorrow and oversee everything. I'll pay you and all that so your probation officer can see you have a legit job and we don't have any issues out of her."

Joey studied his brother's tense body language. "Aight bet. Everything cool?"

Indie rolled his lips over another and bounced his eyes from Taj to Joey. "Let me talk to her and I'll get up with you in a few."

Joey nodded his head and walked away from them. Leading Taj into the room, Indie closed the door and sat on the edge of the bed. Taj was hoping that he was going to tell her everything she was wasn't to know but she knew that wouldn't be the case.

"What's going on, Indie?" Taj asked pulling her bottom lip between her teeth as she looked at him. Slumped shoulders, irritation was present and it had a hint of disappointment and worry. There were things that Indie was living with that she knew he would never come out and tell her.

"Baby," he muttered shaking his head coming out of his hand. "They just wanted to know about some hood shit."

"Okay..."

"That's it," Indie said and Taj shook her head. "I said that's it."

"But that's not it, Indie. I know it's not. Don't leave me in the dark, please tell me something." She damn near pleaded for him to open up more than he'd already done.

Indie took a deep breath and looked up at her. "Baby, I said that's it. There's shit I'm going to tell you without an issue and then there's shit that you don't need to know. What I got going on with them isn't something you need to be in."

Taj was not feeling the response Indie was giving her. In fact, her face scrunched up into a ball and her hands fused themselves onto her hips. "Why not, Indigo?"

Indie dropped his head, chuckled softly, and mumbled something to himself. That only made Taj's face got tighter. "I thought that street shit was over?"

"Baby, I will always be a nigga from the streets. I will always be a Crip. How I move away from the shit is all that should matter right now. It's a part of me but it's not who I am. You got to trust me when I tell you that it's nothing you should be in. If you know, that makes you responsible. I've told you once and I'll tell you a million more times, I'm supposed to protect you. You knowing everything that I did ain't protection, it makes you a target. Just relax. I'm home and everything is cool." Indie's answer wasn't enough to fill her up but it was enough to pacify her.

Taj let her face relax and licked her dry lips. "I don't like it but okay. Just promise me this..."

"What can I do to make this easier?"

"Promise me that you won't shut me out of everything. You're not the only one living in your world anymore," Taj mumbled looking at him stand to his feet as the doorbell rang. She could read the uneasiness in his face – she could feel it. It made her stomach do somersaults and her mouth go dry.

Indie opened the room door and shouted down the hall, "Joey, I got it!"

"Aight!" Joey shouted back.

"Indie..." Taj captured his attention briefly before he could walk out.

"Baby, I promise."

She groaned in annoyance as he shot down the hall toward the door. Running her hand over the back of her neck, Taj closed her eyes and focused on her breathing so her nerves could settle. She tried to tell herself that it would be okay and she needed to adjust to who Indie was, a grown ass man. He never let her in on what was going on before and that wasn't going to change no matter how much she huffed and puffed about it. There wasn't any need for her to make a big deal about it either. Taj knew that there was information that he would always keep from her. With a heavy sigh, Taj opened her eyes and looked around the room.

"Taj, get yourself together," she said to herself before she heard Diane's voice float into the house.

"Why are you opening the door like that, boy?" Diane questioned. "Indigo, don't play with me. Put that gun away. Where is your brother?"

"In his room, I thought you were... never mind." Indie's voice floated back in the room after his mothers'. "That's all that's important to you?"

"Indie, your brother has been in jail eating that nasty food and trying not to drop the soap and be new booty. I'm over here to feed him," Diane said in a matter of fact tone causing Indie to rumble in laughter and call for Joey to come out.

Taj finished pulling herself together and walked down the hall to greet Diane. "Hey, Ms. Diane."

Diane's mouth went from about to shoot a comment at Indie to a wide smile seeing Taj saunter down the hall past Indie. Taj was wrapped up in Diane's arms and returned the gesture. "Let me find out..."

Indie grinned watching the long embrace between his mother and Taj. "She's staying for a couple of days."

"So, it's safe to say that you two have worked everything out and I can tell Senior he lost?" Diane teased letting go of Taj and shifting her attention from Taj to Indie. The mention of Senior's name made both of them roll their eyes.

"Anyway," Taj started up breaking the tension in the room. "What are you cooking?"

"Baby, you can't cook," Diane laughed.

"Is it too late to learn? I kind of missed those lessons," Taj admitted. The thought of her mother hit her like a bag of bricks. Stopping for a second to reset herself and trying to hide how it affected her, she hummed and tucked her hair behind her ears. "She was gone before we could have those vital lessons."

Diane's eyes were soft. She looked over Taj and let her lips turn up at the corners. With a nod of the head she placed the bags on the counter. "Well, that will change altogether. We're just making spaghetti. It's easy and it's one of Indie's favorites. Make sure he cooks for you one of these days."

"I'll be cooking every day," Indie spoke up teasing Taj. "I am not going to risk it."

He reached out to pull her into him and kissed the top of her head. Something quick to reassure her that they were good. "You good, Baby?"

"I'm good," Taj replied not looking up at him but he made her. Lightly grabbing her chin and tilting it upward he repeated himself.

"You good, Baby?"

"I'm good," Taj hummed as Indie pressed his lips against her. "Sorry for pressing the issue."

"Ain't no need to be sorry. I'm not goin' to have you out here worrying. Just know that whatever needs to be handled, I'll handle it." His voice was low enough for her to hear and Diane to strain her ears to hear. "Relax, aight?"

"Aight," Taj mimicked him making him laugh and kiss her lips one more time before letting her go.

"She's all yours, Ma. If she doesn't learn anything, I'm blaming you," Indie teased before starting out the kitchen to find Joey.

"I'm happy you two are finally on the same page."

Taj cleared her throat and helped Diane unpack the groceries. "I just want to stay on the same page."

"That's what that was all about? Remember this, he will treat you right, love you, but just because he traded in his khakis and chucks for a suit doesn't mean that he still doesn't live by the code of the streets. He won't tell you everything you want to know, but he will tell you everything you need to know."

"I know, I just have to get accustomed to it again," Taj admitted. "He's different."

"And so are you. Enjoy getting to know him as who he is right now. It's a fresh start for the garden to bare new flowers."Taj tied her hair up and dived into her cooking lesson with Diane. It felt good to have someone older to lean on. Although she missed her mother more and more as she was coming into her own womanhood, she appreciated the role that Aunt Mary and Diane had taken on in her life. Diane made sure to keep Taj close, not because Taj loved her son but because she loved Taj.

She threw the vegetables into the pan of olive oil and looked over at Diane who was focused on seasoning the ground beef just right. "Thank you."

"There is no need to thank me, Baby. I already told you, you're one of mine too. I loved you from the minute you walked through my door. Nothing is going to change that, not even your daddy."

Taj scoffed. "Let's not even bring him up."

Diane stopped what she was doing to look at Taj. "As much as your daddy irritates my soul, just know that he did his best with what he had and forgiving him, isn't for him, it's for you."

She refrained from telling her about his latest stunt and nodded her head. "I hear you loud and clear."

CHAPTER THREE

*I*ndigoIt was ten in the morning and Taj was stirring around the kitchen with Joey attempting to make pancakes. Indie watched from the patio listening to the ocean with a blunt burning between his lips. Taj's crash cooking course the night before was hilarious. Indie couldn't help but chuckle at the flashback from the night before and the added comedy from watching her try to perfect the pancake batter now. Joey's face was rooted in disbelief while he poured the lumpy batter out down the sink.

"Baby," he groaned. "Thank God you're pretty."

Taj's brows pinned together and she huffed throwing her hands up in the air. "Apparently I can't do everything. Can't say I didn't try, though."

"You did, thank you." Joey chuckled lightly. "Just stick to computers and shit 'cause this ain't it."

"The hate!" Taj laughed closing up the pancake box. "I don't appreciate this attack."

Indie inhaled the last of his blunt and blew the smoke out

into a cloud around him before walking back into the house to kiss Taj's face. "I think you should stick with coding."

Taj smacked her lips and rolled her eyes making Indie laugh. "All I'm sayin' is you probably can create an app where you can cook in that...only. Because real food isn't your forte and it's cool, Baby."

"You got jokes, I see. Both of y'all do. It's cool though, I'm good at everything else." Taj grabbed a glass of water and hopped on the counter.

Positioning himself between her thighs, Indie kissed the curve of her chin and placed his hands on her hips. "That's a fuckin' fact. Look, we'll grab something to eat on the way...go get dressed."

With her eyebrows raised and her bottom lip being gnawed on by her teeth, Taj spoke in a low tone. "Is everything a demand?"

"You gave into those demands last night when you were scream—"

Joey spoke up. "Yeah about that... I'm really going to need both of y'all to keep it down."

Taj's face flushed red and Indie snickered after kissing Taj's lips. "You need some headphones or somethin'? I'm makin' up for lost time."

Taj slapped Indie on the shoulder and giggled at the kiss he placed to her collarbone. "I'm sorry, Jojo. Where are we going?"

"Ridin' around. Dress comfortable." With one last kiss to her face, Indie stepped back and let her hop down. He couldn't let her pass him without a smack to the ass that caused her to clamp down on her lip and look over her shoulder at him.

"Y'all have no damn shame," Joey grunted pouring a giant bowl of cereal. "I'm still standin' here. Just because I've accepted this betrayal don't mean I'm cool with it."

Indie ignored him and watched Taj walk out the kitchen

and down the hall. A soft lust filled grunt left his lips and a smirk took over his face before he pulled himself out of all the salacious thoughts running around his mind and refocused on Joey. "How you feelin', nigga?"

Joey shrugged his shoulders and leaned on the counter. "I feel like I fucked up some shit and I need to figure out how to get back on track now that this shit is going to follow me for a minute."

Indie leaned on the other side of the counter and studied his brothers slumped body posture. "Stand up straight and poke your chest out nigga," Indie commanded looking at his brother. "You ain't been through or did shit that I haven't done. You got to take your wins and your losses as a man. Stand tall in that shit and hold your head up. I could beat it into your head how much you fucked up, but for what? That shit ain't going to change nothin'. You fucked up, got caught slippin' but I bet that shit won't ever happen again. Now your head is on a swivel, now you gotta maneuver different. Now you got to find another means of stacking your bread. I'm giving you the tools but you got to take that shit and make it your own. I want you to work with Ricky and get all the building shit straightened out."

"I appreciate it, bro," Joey spoke up standing upright and reaching out to Indie to pull him into an embrace. "Don't tell nobody I like your tall ass."

Indie's laughter rumbled against the wall and he let Joey go. "Ask the streets, I don't like your ass either."

"They know better...you good?" Joey questioned. "You look like you got something on your head."

"Man..." Indie muttered running his hand down his face. "You want to hear some funny shit..."

"I got a feeling that what you're about to tell ain't going to be funny." Joey leaned down on the counter and started eating his cereal. "Make me laugh."

"That nigga Ricky...acquired more product and was out here pushing it after I said I cut the shit. I'm really starting to think that pops was a rolling stone for real because you and that nigga Ricky act a fuckin' like. That's the funny shit." Indie waved his finger and chuckled lightly. "You two both got hard ass heads."

"Shit, you always said that was family though," Joey said followed by a laugh. "How are you going to move?"

"The same way I moved with you. Y'all grown men now and I ain't your daddy. It's on you to figure out how you movin'. I gave y'all the keys...I gave y'all the way, I'm stepping back. Y'all either ridin' and trustin' me or not. I'm not fightin' no nigga to better his life," Indie rumbled followed by a suck of his front two teeth. "Anyway, you can make sure that these contractors stay on time. I got to focus on the tech center."

"I got you, do whatever you got to do," Joey assured him. Indie welcomed the change in him. Jail seemed to set Joey on the right path. He didn't want that route for Ricky. He knew that if Ricky got jammed up everything would be on Ajai. He didn't want that for either of them, he could only hope that his speech went further.

Hearing his bedroom door close brought him out of his thoughts. Looking up to see Taj walk down the hall, Indie looked back at Joey and threw his hand up. "I'll be back later. "

"Aight, bro."

Indie stepped out the kitchen and grabbed his keys. "You ready?"

"Yeah, just wondering where we're going..." she muttered walking past him out the house.

"Out, ridin'."

"Riding where?"

"Down the street."

"Down the street to what and are there snacks?" Taj

continued to question him stopping at the driveway and looking up at Indie batting her eyelashes.

He couldn't help but smile. That's what she did to him, turned him into putty with just a bat of the eyes and a touch. Indie traced his bottom lip with his tongue before unlocking the car. "Get in the car, girl."

"Mm," Taj hummed. "Talk to me nice."

Indie opened her door and smacked her on the ass as she climbed in and looked down at her. "All these damn questions."

"And no damn answers," Taj rebutted pulling the seatbelt across her body.

"Listen, what happened to the good ol days when you just got in the car without all these questions and attitude?" he joked getting settled in the driver's seat and hit the button to start. He was expecting her reply with a smart comment. The only thing Taj was doing was writing a check for later that he was going to cash happily.

Taj smacked her lips and looked at him before countering his question with, "Some dumb ass niggas thought it was fun to shoot the car up."

Indie reached over and gripped her thigh through her jeans. "You don't got to worry about that shit no more. That's been handled."

That must have been enough to pacify her because she placed her hand on top of his and started scrolling through her emails with her free hand. Indie welcomed the silence so he could let his mind trail off on everything he needed to do to get the center up and running.

Pulling up at the high school, he killed the engine and looked over at Taj. "You ready?"

"Why are we at a school?" Taj looked at her phone and pushed the door open.

Indie got out, shut his door, and walked over to her side

with a smirk. "Letting you in. Like I said, there's shit I'm not going to be sharing with you, but this, you got the keys to. Come on."

Taj followed Indie into the school and walked down the hall to a computer room where there were twenty kids broken up in groups of fours. They were building computers, programming, brainstorming, and collaborating with each other with smiles on their faces.

"Wow," Taj released with a whistle and a smile spread across her face just from seeing how happy the kids were. "Who is running this program? Where is the funding coming from?"

Taj started walking through the room to take a closer look at what they were working on. Indie followed behind her while talking to the kids, introducing her and suggesting different ways for them to solve their problems. "Right now, I'm funding it. They meet here every Saturday. It keeps them off the streets, it's safe and it's something they love doing."

Indie stopped at the desk in front of the room and Taj stood by him. It was second nature for him to drape his arm over her shoulder and kiss the top of her head. The pride that Taj felt because Indie was making strides to really make his dream come true exuded through her pores. "Talk to me."

Taj looked up at Indie with a tender look in her eyes. She locked her fingers between his and smiled letting her dimples pierce her cheeks. "I am so proud of you, baby. You're doing everything you said you were going to do."

He smiled wide and nodded his head looking around the room at the kids busy at work. "This what it's all about for me. What it's always been about finding a way out and passing that off. I've seen everyone around me lose someone to the streets and it has to stop somewhere. If I can get five of them, I won."

Taj kissed the back of his knuckles before she broke away

from him and walked over the group of girls who were coding on one of the old computers. Indie dove into the other groups and started helping them. The time flew by and it was almost four in the afternoon before Indie and Taj realized that it was time to get them home. Taj made sure they had something to eat before they went home. Indie relished in the fact that Taj lit up around them and she enjoyed sharing her passion with them. Making a mental note to do this again with her, they closed up the building and headed to get dinner.

CHAPTER FOUR

*T*aj
After making sure all the kids got home, Taj climbed into the passenger seat of the car and kicked her feet up on the dashboard. She couldn't describe the feeling that took over her body. What she knew was that she needed this feeling to stay around longer. She enjoyed feeling like she was making a difference and she enjoyed being happy.

Happy.

It had been so long since she'd truly been happy. Although she wasn't expecting her life to take the turns it did, she was smiling again. She was looking forward to what the next day held, and most off all, her heart was beating again. It all felt surreal.

She watched as the houses faded into the background and the city lights took over as Indie maneuvered through the traffic. Taj glanced over at him and smiled. Then, she reached out and touched the side of his face. Indie wrapped her hand in his and kissed it. "A penny for your thoughts."

Taj rolled her lips against one another and hummed before

she looked away. She glared out the window with her hand still held in Indigo's custody. She didn't want it back. She remembered the times where she longed to feel his touch and now that she had it back, she never wanted to be without it. Tomorrow she would be back in San Francisco wanting to feel him all over so she held on to this moment and remained silent a little while longer.

Indie didn't say anything else, he just waited for Taj to return her attention from her thoughts to him. She looked back at him with a tender look in her eyes and adored how he held onto her hand giving her a silent gesture of protection while keeping his eyes on the road. Although Indie was different, he was hers and the heart that beat inside his chest was familiar.

"I'm proud of you," Taj finally broke her silence. She watched as he smirked and shifted in his seat. "Even though you might've gone off course you still came back and did everything you said you were going to do. Not everyone does that...not everyone can bounce back like you did."

"I was determined. Determination will make a man do shit that he said he was never going to do again. It'll make him push himself harder than he ever did. I was determined to get back to you. I got to be real though, for a minute, I thought that I wasn't going to get back to you. I wasn't okay with that. I gave you my heart and I never wanted it back, what I wanted was the home I left it in." Indigo's words made Taj's lips turn up into a smile.

"You know..." she replied with a huff. "I prayed for this. For you. For us. And our dreams. Even though I was mad as hell at God for taking you from me, I still prayed just to get through it."

"Did He answer you?" Indie rose his brow and glanced over at her. She nodded her head.

"He sure did...He's not done yet, though." Turning her head to look out the window she inhaled and looked at him.

Exhaling and gathering her thoughts. "You know that investment is yours if you still need it."

Indie scoffed lightly in amusement. His reaction threw her for a loop. Taj couldn't read his expression. "I impressed you with that shit back there didn't I?"

"To be honest, I am blown away. What you're doing is amazing and it's needed. Seeing how those kids faces lit up when you walked in and how they listened when you talked. They deserve a better tech center than they have," Taj gushed with pride over Indie's persistence to do exactly what he set out to do.

"Look," Indigo started. "I don't want you to feel like you're obligated to give me anything because we're together. That's not what I want."

"Me neither...you deserve that investment, babe," Taj countered.

"Okay," Indie spoke up approaching a stop light. "Come a few more times and then decide what you're going to do. But I don't want you to do it because I'm -- what the fuck?"

Indie's entire expression changed as blue lights flashed behind him. Instantly, Taj's breath hitched. She quickly looked around the car to make sure there wasn't anything she could see.

"Be cool, it's in the glove box," Indie instructed her. "Don't move fast, just sit there and be cool aight?"

"Okay," Taj's voice was no higher than a whisper while Indie pulled into the gas station. Indie let her hand go and watched the mirrors to see two cops walk around with their guns drawn. "Indie..."

"Baby, be cool," he instructed before he rolled his window down. His face glowed red and his mouth was tight.

"Get your ass out the car!" one shouted at him as the other

flashed his flashlight in Taj's face. Indie did as he was told and looked at the two.

"Look, y'all not about to do this shit with my girl in the car," he growled flashing a warning glare at both of them. "You don't roll up on me like this."

Taj could hear him from her seat inside the car since he left the door open. "Y'all know better than this shit. You want me you know how to get me but what we're not going to do is this tonight. You know where I'm from, you know how I get down, homie. What y'all want from me?"

Indie leaned on the trunk of the car and crossed his arms. His back was turned to the rear-view mirror on purpose. He didn't want to upset Taj or make her worry but she was on the verge of feeling both. His voice got lower while the three of them exchanged words. Whatever Indie was saying to them was causing them to back off and leave him alone.

The last thing Taj could make out before Indie climbed back into the car was, "You got lucky tonight, but we will be seeing you around. We heard about you."

"You can hear about me all you want nigga. Y'all not going to be rolling up on me with my lady in the car. That's never going to happen. If you want me, come get me the right way, not like this. You understand me?"

The officers chuckled and walked away to their cruiser and turned their lights off.

Indie waited until they were gone before he pulled out of the gas station and avoided Taj's eyes on his face. "Should I even ask?"

"No," Indie answered simply. "Not at all."

With a heavy sigh Taj played with her fingers in her lap before nodding her head.

"Alright," Taj muttered.

She would talk to him about this later when his jaw wasn't

clenched and his grip on the steering wheel wasn't tight. They were going to talk about this because being shut out of parts of his world wasn't something that she wanted to live with. For Indie to pick and choose what he shared with her was just as damaging as not being there at all.

Indie could feel the tension building and decided to break it before it ruined the night. "Baby, it was nothing. These cops think I'm out to make trouble for them. That's not the case and that's all that was about. Can we get dinner and have a good night before you leave me tomorrow? That's all I want."

Taj swallowed the lump in her throat and pushed her concerns to the back burner. "Okay, Indie."

"Thank you, Baby."

JHENE AIKO: BLUE DREAM

Don't wake me up 'cause I'm in love with all that you are
You make me see the truth in things, I think that you are
The remedy for everything, it seems that you are
The truth itself 'cause nothing else can me so far

CHAPTER FIVE

$\mathcal{M}$aria
   Strolling through the office with her purse slung over her shoulder and a smile across her face, Maria grabbed some papers off the admin's desk, a bagel and container of cream cheese out the break room and headed into her office. Lately, it seemed like everything was going right in her life. Her siblings were taken care of, her grandmother was in good health and her love life was off the Richter scale. The last thing Maria excepted when she moved to San Francisco was to meet a man that would change her outlook on everything. For the first time in her life, she felt a love she'd never experienced before. Now that she had, she didn't want to let it go. It was worth protecting at all costs.

   This is how Taj must've felt. That simple thought made her frown a bit before closing her office door. "I haven't heard from her since she left."

   Maria got settled behind her desk, powered up her MacBook and started preparing her bagel. Once it was powered up, she Facetime'd Taj hoping that she wouldn't be tied up in anything that wouldn't allow them to have a quick conversation. A few rings sounded out and Indie's face graced the screen.

"What's up, Maria?" Indie asked with his signature smile. "How you doin'?"

"I'm great. You look like you are too." Maria chuckled watching Indigo sit up and flash the phone over to Taj's back.

"She's usually up by now, but I figured I'd let her sleep. I know when she gets back up there she's going to running a mile a minute." Indie grunted softly as he shuffled down the hall and looked over his shoulder every so often.

Maria bit into her bagel and nodded her head. "You're right about that. You ready to give me my friend back?"

"Hell no," Indie dragged out. "I'm trying to hold her ass hostage. But I know she got big things going on up there and I can't be selfish. Look, it's a good thing you called, I need you to do something for me."

"Whatever you need I got you," Maria quickly fired off excited to be a part of Indie doing something special for Taj.

"I need you to set up a date night for us. Whatever she likes I want it," Indie started hearing his bedroom door open. "She's up, I'll text you the rest of the details."

"Why aren't you in the bed?" Taj's groggy voice filled the space. Maria could see her peek over Indie's shoulder and see Maria. "Hey friend. What are you two in here conspiring about?"

"We were just talking about how much we love you. So much that we wanted you to sleep." Maria snickered making Taj's eyes roll after she looked at both of them. Maria's snicker made Indie shrug his shoulders before he handed the phone over to her and kissed her lips.

"I just wanted to make sure everything was good." Indie smirked before grabbing a handful of her ass from under her shirt. Taj flashed him a seductive look before he walked out of Maria's sight.

"You two are nasty," Maria spoke up once Indie was gone. "I hope you're making up for lost time."

"I sure as hell am." Taj clamped down on her lip and took a seat on the couch. "How's everything going? You miss me yet?"

"Well that's evident but I know you need this. Everything is running like it should be. And I am perfectly fine," Maria responded with a smile that grew wider by the second.

"Ohh, somebody must be making you very happy," Taj responded in a sing a long voice and Maria's eyes fully disappeared behind her cheeks.

"You know...I get it now," Maria confessed dropping her eyes from the screen. "Here's my confession as your best friend... I understood what you were going through from a logical standpoint but I didn't understand it from an emotional one. I just knew that you loved someone enough to hold on to every last thread of them. Now that I'm deeply in like...I don't want to lose that."

"Maria," Taj crooned looking at the screen and seeing Maria lift her head.

"I'm sorry for not getting it. I get it now. That's really why I wanted to call you. Also, to tell you to enjoy it. I know sometimes you get into your head and you want to know everything and try to fix everything but please just live for right now and love for right now." Maria's eyes were soft as she looked at Taj's face that was just as soft as hers. "We're having a moment. I need you to cry too bitch."

Taj laughed and wiped the lone tear that fell from her eyes. "I don't understand why you're apologizing to me. You stuck with me through all of it and I didn't make it easy. You deserve every shred of happiness that life has for you. This is the happiest I've ever seen you and it looks good on you. I am mad that you made me have this moment so damn early in the morning, though."

"I would be having it with you here, but somebody is getting their back blown out day in and day out." Maria giggled. "And don't even tell me that you aren't. That good dick glow is all around you."

"Well," Taj dragged out with a smirk. "It's been a minute. But it's been more than that. We went to the tech center at the high school the other day and, Maria, I'm blown away. They wanted to be there and they didn't want to leave."

"So, you've considered giving him the investment?"

"I am giving him the investment. That's not a question. I don't think I was ever not going to give it to him. That center has been his dream for the longest and who am I to stand in the way of that?" Taj pushed her curly hair out her face and glanced back down the hall.

"I know that, look," Maria commented seeing that look in Taj's eyes again. "I'm going to let you two go."

"I'll see you." Taj blew her a kiss and disconnected the call.

Exiting out the screen, Maria started shifting through emails and her to-do list. She took a second to enjoy the feeling of completeness that was coursing through her body. With a lighthearted sigh she sat up and started to tackle her to do list.

After ten minutes of sorting through applicant's a soft knock graced her door. "Maria?" The admin popped her head in and looked at her.

"What's up?"

"Uh Malcolm is here and he won't leave until he speaks to Taj. I've told him that she's not here but..."

"I got it," Maria spoke up standing to her feet. Reaching under her desk to grab her bat, she marched out of the office to the front desk where Malcolm stood with bruises over his face.

Maria couldn't help but chuckle. "It looks like someone got to you before I could."

"Where is she?"

"That's none of your concern anymore, Malcolm. You're looking real dehydrated right now like a crazy ex. It will be better for you if you just leave." Maria's warning was clear as she laid the bat over her shoulders. "This is a place of business and I would like to keep it that way so...you should go now, or I can make you go."

Malcolm growled and looked Maria up and down. "You tell her when you see her that I'm not done with her yet and I want everything that was promised to me."

"Or what? Two more rings around your eyes and castration? Nigga get the fuck out of here," Maria spat turning to walk away. "Call security and get him out of here."

CHAPTER SIX

*T*aj "Ball, ball, ball," Ricky shouted to Indie for a pass. Indie took the shot and missed. Taj winced lowly at how bad Indie missed the shot.

"I'm glad they're just playing against some kids because this is terrible," Taj muttered to herself.

She leaned back on the bleachers with her legs crossed at the ankles and arms resting on the seat behind her for support. Indie, Joey, and Ricky ran back and forth on the court playing the second pick up game of the day with the neighborhood kids. Some of them she met at the tech center the day before and a few others were younger. Taj's heart grew larger with love for Indie, the more she discovered about him. Although he'd kept things from her in the name of protecting her, all the good things he was doing had her overlooking the things that he didn't want her to know.

Taj glanced over at Bleu being bounced up and down on Ajai's knee as she sang nursery rhymes with her own little remix to make him laugh and keep him from running on the court behind Ricky. Taj couldn't help but smile more and dread having to leave L.A. in a day to go back to the real world that needed her attention.

"Again, Mama," Bleu demanded at the end of the song. Ajai groaned, took a deep breath, and started all over again. Just as she was getting fed up with the same three songs remixed and on repeat, the guys put a pause to their game to get water and catch their breath.

Taj studied Indigo's body language and his refusal to look at Ricky. Even when Ricky said something to him, Indie ignored it. It was evident that something happened between them and that could have been the reason Indie was so tight lipped.

"Hey, Bleu," Ricky came over and started tickling Bleu while pulling him off of Ajai's leg. "Let's give mommy a break."

Ricky put Bleu down and let him run across the court to the other kids. Indie stood off to the side of the court and scrolled through his phone before waving Joey over to him.

"Ajai," Taj spoke grabbing Ajai's attention from Ricky and Bleu. "What's going between these two?"

Ajai looked at the distance between Indie and Ricky and huffed. "They're probably fighting again. They've been like this for the last four years on and off. Ricky would do something Indie didn't like and they would get spicy and then vice versa. So ain't no telling what they're fighting over. Just like Indie doesn't tell you anything, neither does Ricky. I am on a need to know basis."

Taj twisted her face and rolled her eyes. "I hate that shit. Tell me everything and let me figure out how I'm going to deal with it. This secret keeping irritates the shit out of me."

Ajai scoffed and nodded her head in agreement. "You ain't lying. Especially with these two. They can be mad as hell with one another but they aren't going to ever tell their secrets."

"Well that is evident," Taj replied rolling her eyes.

Ajai let silence fall between them before she glanced over at Indie, Joey, and Ricky one last time before she asked, "How much longer do I have you?"

"Tonight, and tomorrow, I'll fly out on Tuesday and go see about this business. I've been out the loop and I can only imagine how much stuff has piled up on my desk," Taj shared pushing the flyaway's out of her face.

"Hmm," Ajai hummed before looking back at Taj. "Are you going to see your dad before you leave?"

Taj didn't answer. In fact, Taj didn't flinch a muscle. It made Ajai laugh, knowing that Taj heard exactly what she asked but chose to play deaf and mute. "Taj, you heard me."

"Huh? You said something?" Taj questioned glancing at Ajai. "I'm sorry what were you saying?"

"Girl," Ajai laughed. "You heard me. I asked you if you were going to see your dad while you were here."

"I have nothing to say to him. Not hi or bye. I literally have nothing to say to him. I don't know when I'll be ready to talk to him but it's not right now."

"You know," Ajai started up with a sigh. "He loves you. His way of showing it needs some work though."

"Some?" Taj screeched causing Indie to look up at her.

"Baby, you good?" he questioned examining her with a tender expression.

Taj nodded her head. "Yeah, I'm good."

"Aight," Indie nodded before turning back around and finishing his conversation with Joey.

"Senior needs a lot of whatever it is. I don't have it for him. I don't have the patience nor the remorse for him anymore. If he loved me like he swore up and down that he did, he wouldn't have put me through half the shit that he did..."

"Ay, Baby," Indie spoke up butting into their conversation. "Y'all want to see the commercial buildings?"

Taj nodded her head and sat up. "Yeah, y'all are done?"

"Ricky just bought them ice cream. Another game ain't happening today," he chuckled walking up the bleachers to hold his hand out to help both Ajai and Taj up.

"Thanks bro. We'll meet you there." Ajai smirked watching Indie throw his arm over Taj's shoulder and walk down the bleachers by her.

Gathering up all of their things, they headed toward the building complex. "I want you to see what we've been working on. I like that look in your face when you see what I've been doing."

"Pride?" Taj questioned with a grin. "Duh, you're doing this shit. That's what makes me happy...you're coming up but you're not leaving the hood and you're not leaving the people that you came up with."

"I could never do that," Indie shared. "I wanted to. I wanted to get the fuck out and when I did, I felt guilty as shit. There were people here that needed some hope and someone to look up to. And it just so happened that it was me. I'm going to do whatever I have to do to show them a better way. Think about I came up off serving the curb, getting shot and coming back to the same streets. If that's not a reason to go and get it I don't know what is."

It was something about the way that Indie spoke that made Taj listen. Even when she didn't want to. Not only did it make her listen but it made her take in every word that he spoke. The baritone of his voice, the passion in his eyes and the purpose of his life that he spoke into the atmosphere; she loved every vibration of it. That was probably the reason she couldn't keep herself off of him.

"You got that look in your eye, Baby," Indie chuckled grabbing her thigh.

"I can't help it. Listening to you talk with so much passion makes me wish I wasn't sweaty and didn't wear panties."

Indie's chuckle formed into a full-blown laugh. "Baby, don't none of that shit matter to me. I'll devour it like it's a cookie. You know that shit."

"I be knowin'," Taj replied. "You're going to be able to survive without me for a couple weeks?"

"Who said I'm not going to pull up on you?" Indie countered. "I'm not about to let you out my sight that long especially with that nigga still runnin' around."

Taj rolled her eyes and smacked her lips. "Wasn't nobody thinking about him. Trust me."

"Oh yeah?"

"Oh yeah. Your name is all over me anybody can see that."

Indie grunted, pulling into the parking lot of the commercial buildings and looking around. "Keep talking that shit, baby."

"I plan on it," she hummed looking around the lot.

"They got this shit cleaned up nice," Indie muttered killing the engine and climbing out of the car. He quickly adjusted himself and looked back at Taj. "You got my shit on brick and I can't do shit about it."

"It is very clear to me that you two freaks forgot I was sitting back here," Joey spoke up making Indie and Taj look at each other before smiling.

"My bad, bro," Indie apologized.

"I'm going to get my own car. I can't keep doing this shit," Joey muttered getting out the car and walking toward the building.

Taj giggled, got out the car, and climbed on the trunk

waiting for Ricky and Ajai to pull up. Indie leaned on the trunk and looked up at her. "What's on your mind?"

"You and Ricky need to work out whatever you got going on. I'll look at the building later. You two work it out."

"Taj," Indie groaned before she pulled him into her and kissed his lips tenderly.

"Take care of it so when you come to bed tonight the load is less, okay?"

"Aight. You got it."

Taj nodded her head and smiled at him. "I'll go home with Ajai."

"And be naked when I get there."

Taj shook her head no. "I like when you work for it."

CHAPTER SEVEN

*S*enior

"Not today," he huffed.

He parked his car in front of Mary's house and released a heavy sigh. Senior already thought it was weird that Mary had called him asking that he come over and fix something. She normally was self-sufficient and rarely asked for help, so he knew this was a set up. And when he rolled down her street and saw Diane's car in the driveway, his assumptions were proven to be right. Pushing himself back in his seat he closed his eyes and tried to calm his nerves before he walked into the house. Diane or Indie weren't on his list of favorite people. But now that Taj had made her decision it would be difficult to get rid of them. He had done everything that he thought of to keep them apart but still they found their way back to each other.

"Some freaking divine intervention huh?" he grumbled to himself. Senior turned the car off and pushed the door open. "Might as well get this shit over with."

A few jumps, crack of the neck and poke out of the chest, Senior was ready to enter the war zone known as Diane Sims.

He didn't want to argue with her today, he really didn't feel like it. He'd been avoiding her like Taj was ducking and dodging him. He traveled up the stairs to the house and let himself in.

"Alright, Mary," he released walking further inside. "Let's get this over with."

"What a way to start," Diane mumbled to herself but she was loud enough for Senior to hear her and cause him to contort his face.

Instead of saying something smart in return, Senior took a seat and looked at his sister. "I'm tired, let's get this over with."

"Maybe you should start by saying sorry," Diane spoke up making Senior scoff. "You're more of a child than I thought you were, Charles."

"Why the hell would you call my daughter and entice her to come back here when I tried so damn hard to keep her away?" Senior questioned.

Diane rolled her eyes and pursed her lips together. "Your daughter is a grown ass woman, let's start there. A grown ass woman that we all lied to. I wanted to make sure she knew the truth before she decided to close the chapter."

"Hm," Senior buzzed with his mouth closed. He couldn't help but think about the what if. What if he'd told her the truth from the beginning? Maybe they wouldn't be going through this. Maybe she would actually be talking to him now.

Mary sat in her chair and looked at both of them consumed with their own thoughts. Senior's face wore the sadness of being shut out of Taj's life. He had dark circles around his eyes from not sleeping and his shoulders slumped over.

"She hasn't talked to you?" Mary asked.

Senior shook his head no. "She told me to stay out her business."

"Oh, Chucky," Mary's voice was full of remorse.

Senior lifted his hand off his lap and waved his hand in the air. "She's not mad about that anymore..."

"Oh my God," Diane threw her hands up in the air. "What have you done?"

Saying it out loud meant that he would have to accept the fact that he messed up in the worst of ways. He dropped his head back and massaged his temples.

"What did you do, Chucky?" Mary's voice resounded through the living room.

Senior sucked in all the air he could before he released it. "I pushed Malcolm into proposing and marrying her for a stake in her company..."

Diane damn near blew the roof off when she said, "You did what!"

Diane's breathing intensified like she was a bull that was being taunted by a red cape. Senior could feel her outrage from across the room. She was well within her right of feeling a certain way about how he mismanaged the entire situation.

"I know, I know," Senior groaned still massaging his temples. His pride wouldn't let him tell them the hell that Taj was going through silently with Malcolm. That would've resulted in lectures about how badly he'd fucked this up with his daughter. He didn't want to hear what he knew especially from Diane.

"Chucky, I wish I had some sound advice for you but I don't," Mary shared with a shake of the head. "I don't know how you're going to fix this one. Taj has grown into her own woman and the last thing you want is for her to move on with her life without you in it."

"I know," Senior muttered against his hand that rested on his chin.

"You might not want to hear this, but the only way back to Taj is through Indie," Diane spoke up causing Senior to cut his eyes at her. "I'm not being funny either, Charles. I'm being serious. As much as you two don't care for each other, he's going to be the only one to talk her into it."

"She has a point," Mary agreed. "She's been back for almost a week and hasn't even sent you a bat signal."

"I'm not going through anyone to talk to my daughter."

"Then I guess you won't be talking to your daughter," Diane said with a shrug of her shoulders. She pushed herself up and collected her things. "Before I go, I will apologize for my part in this. You're her father and the love you have for her is limitless and it causes you to behave like a lunatic. But I love her too, and I love her for my son even more. If you just got over yourself you would see that Indie is full of love. He gives it and he requires it. Baby is in great hands."

Senior sat up and rested his elbows against his knees and nodded his head. "Diane, you may be right. But the probability of her hearing me out whether or not I go through Indie is low."

"Well, you got work to do. If need help you know where to find me. But knowing you..." Diane trialed off.

Mary picked up right where Diane stopped. "That probably won't happen because you are stubborn as hell and so is she."

"Exactly," Diane cosigned before saying her goodbyes and leaving.

Mary looked over at Senior and asked, "What happened?"

"What didn't happen?" Senior answered her question with one of his own. "I thought she was in good hands with Malcolm...it seemed like she was."

"When did it seem like that? Every time I saw him, he was beside himself about something small," Mary replied pinning her brows together in confusion. "You just didn't want to see it."

"You might be right."

"Might be? I know I am, and you're wrong. Whatever he did to her is on your hands just as much as it's on his. Swallow your pride and go talk to Indie."

Senior scoffed with laughter. "I'm not doing that shit. At all."

"Then be without Taj. Miss all the happy moments in her life because you couldn't be a man, put your pride aside, and say you messed up. It's not hard, Chucky," Mary said.

"Mm." Senior pushed himself up from his seat and headed to the door. "I'm not talking to that boy about anything that pertains to my daughter."

"That's a bad decision...that boy knows more about your daughter than you do," Mary added as Senior walked out the door mumbling to himself.

"I'm not playing this game with none of them." Climbing back inside his car he growled lowly. "That's my daughter, what I say goes."

CHAPTER EIGHT

Indie

"What up, nigga?" Indie questioned. He was perched on the trunk of his car with a blunt between his lips and a bottle in his hand. His eyes flashed over to Ricky who was climbing out his car. Indie blew the smoke from his lungs up into the air added to the cloud that was already there.

Ricky tightened his jaw and watched as Ajai and Taj exchanged words and giggles before they pulled off and disappeared down the street. "Ain't shit...you good?"

Indie smirked, hopped down and dragged his eyes around the parking lot before heading into the first office space. Ricky reluctantly pulled himself behind Indie and looked around at the progress. The ceiling was fixed and new light fixtures were put in and the paint was almost dry.

"I'm not good," Indie spoke up with his hands in his pockets. "I'm confused."

Turning around to face Ricky, Indie popped the top on his bottle of Crown took a swig and handed it over to Ricky. "Confused as to why you would go against something I thought we were in agreement with. Not only did you lie, you had Manny lie and cover for you too. Out of everyone in the world I choose to trust and keep close, I never would have thought you would be the nigga to go against the grain."

"Indie...look. It was supposed to be short lived," Ricky announced after a swig of the whiskey. He said it like it was enough validation to calm Indie. It wasn't.

"I don't give a fuck about what it was supposed to be. I said shut the shit down and you still ran with it. Got nigga's all in the mix, moving fuckin' sloppy. Got the police watching every fuckin' move you make for what? For some extra fucking cash when we have more than enough!" Indie's voice bellowed through the building. "And it's not you they want Ricky. They don't give a fuck about you. They want me. I'm the nigga on the choppin' block every time you fuck up! Every fight you start, every dumb ass move you make...it's me!"

"You need to calm the fuck down, nigga," Ricky shouted back causing Indie to shove him backward.

"That calm down shit don't fuckin' work no more! I've been calm, I've been cool, I've been collected and my own fuckin' brothers can't follow simple ass directions." Indie was centimeters away from Ricky's face. He glared at him for a few seconds before backing up. "You know what hurts nigga...that you didn't run this shit by me. That you didn't trust me enough to tell me. Because if it were really money you were hurtin' for I would have looked out. But it wasn't money was it?"

Ricky adjusted his clothing and looked at Indie before answering, "Nah, it wasn't."

"That's what I thought. It was about the power...but with power comes responsibility. With power comes prices on your head not just from these niggas out here...but from police. You ain't made for this shit nigga."

"You saying I'm weak?" Ricky questioned looking at Indie like the enemy and not his brother.

"No," Indie answered. "I'm saying you're thoughtless. You don't think about shit before you do it. It's a weakness but it doesn't make you weak, nigga. What makes you weak is your lack of ownership. Your inability to poke your chest out and own the shit you do. That shit gets you killed and taken from your family."

Ricky looked away and his shoulders dropped. Indie watched as his demeanor began to change. "Poke your chest out nigga! Ain't no need to bitch up now. The point of family is that we look out for each other, right or wrong, good, bad or indifferent. But with that family there is a code, never fold on your family."

"Look, I fucked up. That's on me," Ricky admitted. "Wasn't shit funny about the reason I did it. I just..."

"You were just looking out." Indie cut him off. "I get it, but use your head nigga. That's all. This shit better never happen again. The LAPD is trying to find whatever they can about TK...and the only reason they care so much about that nigga is because he was probably talking to them. I can't risk you being wrapped up in this shit with them. Tell Manny and Rico to shut it down or I'm shutting it down."

"There's no need for it," Ricky spoke up. "It's done."

Indie raised his brow and studied Ricky's face for any hint of dishonesty, he found none. He nodded his head. "Aight then. Drink up nigga, the building is almost done. Joey has new doors and shit coming in tomorrow and a few tenants lined up. Ajai's studio is back here, she has the biggest one."

Indie picked up right where they left off. Ricky was his brother; blood couldn't have made them any closer. Regardless of what they went through, nothing was ever big enough for them to fall completely out.

"Joey you came through with this shit," Ricky chuckled looking around.

"I know I did. Plus, my PO doesn't want to hear that I ain't doin' shit," Joey spoke up coming around the corner. "Happy to see that you two kissed and made up."

"Ajai was going to have my head if I didn't get shit right," Ricky admitted causing Indie to laugh.

"I swear Taj was on that same shit too," Indie's laugh filled the room. "Threaten a nigga's night if I didn't come back with good news."

"Y'all know a break wouldn't hurt," Joey muttered to himself. "You could go a night without keeping everyone up."

"Oh shit," Ricky laughed while Indie playfully swung on Joey. "I was going to say you looked tired."

Joey and Indie playfully wrestled around for a few minutes and broke up. "I don't get no sleep, cuh. None at all."

"Sounds like you need to make sure these buildings are up to par so you get your own spot lil' nigga," Indie replied. "Cause Baby is flying out in a few days...so you know."

"I know, I know. I won't be there."

"Uh huh," Indie chuckled. "You do that."

They spent a few more hours laughing, joking, smoking and remembering their time on the streets. All the trouble Ricky got them into and all the trouble Indie got them out of. Everything felt right for them. Things were constantly propelling forward. Indie's dream for himself and his family.

Indie stood up and stretched. "Come on nigga, before Ajai and Taj start tag teaming our lines."

"Shit, you're right," Ricky and Joey followed suit. "It's late as fuck."

Locking up the building, they got in the car and headed toward Indie's house. They were feeling good, especially Indie.

He felt untouchable. The window's down, music blasting, and blunts were being passed around the car.

Indie pulled off from a green trying to relight the blunt between his lips. "Got damn," he huffed swerving a bit.

"You good nigga?" Joey asked from the back seat.

Getting the blunt lit, Indie continued to drive toward the house faster than usual. Indie didn't even see the cop car until the blue lights flashed in the rear view. "Ah fuck, I'm not going back to jail," Joey whined.

Indie groaned and put his blunt in the ashtray. "Be cool, I got it."

Following protocol Indie, pulled over and pulled his license and registration out and waited for the officer to approach the car. Indie blew the remainder of smoke from his lungs and looked up. "Indigo Sims...we meet again, and this time we have a reason to pull you over. You know the drill, get out."

Indie picked up his blunt and took and deep draft from it before climbing out and blew it in the officer's faces. "This ain't about weed or me speeding. So, what's up?"

"This nigga," Joey blew shaking his head. "He's going to get us shot. Watch."

"Chill out Joey," Ricky muttered.

The younger officer laughed and nodded for his partner to come over. "You're right. But you know how you hook a big fish Indie? Small bait. Jones go and search the car."

Officer Jones bent down and flashed his flashlight in Joey and Ricky's face. "Get out."

Indie glanced back at Ricky and Joey standing on the other side of the car. They didn't say anything but they all knew.

"Weed, money, open container, look at this Mack...we got a gun," Jones chuckled as he sifted through Indie's things. Standing up, he said something to Officer Mack that none of them could make out. Jones and Mack started to laugh amongst themselves before they walked back around to the guys leaning on the car still passing the blunt around.

"Alright...whose shit is this. Don't all speak up at once. I can take one or I can take all of you. And Joey...doesn't this violate your parole? I would hate to call your PO."

"That's not even worth the move," Indie muttered. "All that weed and shit is mine. Y'all want me you got me."

The officers took the bait that Indie gave them. He turned around put his hands behind his back and looked at Ricky. "You know where the bail is and keep Taj cool. I'll be home soon."

Within minutes, Indie was cuffed and escorted to the back of the police car. Ricky knew how to handle this situation, the same way he handled it before. But this time Taj was going to have to be filled in completely and that task was in Indie's hands.

WALE: BLACK BONNIE

Can you be someone I can hide my fears with?
And if they got us on the run, we could still chase our dreams
Black Bonnie
Do you see my Black Bonnie?
Talk to you different, but never extra
She like the fact I get aggressive but never possessive
Bad but modest, man, just staying honest
Black Bonnie Parker

CHAPTER NINE

*A*jai
"Okay, here's my confession," Taj slurred a bit between giggles. Her and Ajai had been up drinking and eating takeout while Bleu slept peacefully in the middle of the guest bedroom bed.

"Tell me," Ajai slurred throwing a fry in her mouth. She needed this girl time to let her hair down and release all the tension she couldn't with Ricky.

Taj dipped the side of her burger in the ketchup and took a bite and continued talking with her mouth full. "I hope Indie comes home ready to pass out. I have been folded into a pretzel every night."

"But you like that shit, don't even front like you don't," Ajai giggled even more. "He's happy to have you back. It's not like he can run out the house and tell everyone how much he misses you and loves you."

"You right," Taj hummed with a smile plastered across her face. "I am not ready to leave I know that."

Ajai frowned her face at the thought of Taj going back to

San Francisco and her ex. The last thing she wanted to happen was for Indie to go to jail behind him. That was an itch that both Ricky and Indie wanted to scratch they were just waiting for the perfect moment to do so.

"I'm not ready for you to leave. I'll be by myself again and doing the same thing day in and day out," Ajai pouted before taking the rest of her drink to the head.

Taj happily hopped down from the stool on the other side of the island and grabbed the bottle of vodka and tonic water off the counter. She spun back around and returned to the island counter with Ajai. Taj wiggled in her seat and refreshed both of their glasses and squeezed a wedge of lime into each.

"This skinny cocktail is good as hell," Ajai groaned into her glass.

Taj wiggled her shoulders and stuck her tongue out and did a silly dance in the stool. "I be knowing how to hook some shit up. Speaking of hooking shit up, please do something to my head before I go."

"I've been waiting for you to ask. I'm too lit to do it now but bihhhh, in the morning I got you." Ajai and Taj both threw their head back and laughed before they lifted their glasses up and clanked it against one another. "Look me in my eyes or seven years of bad sex."

"Oh shit," Taj focused in to Ajai and looked her in the eyes. "The last two of awful sex was enough to..."

Ricky and Joey burst through the door. Ricky took off to Indie's unfinished office to grab the bail money he sat aside. Joey shot by the kitchen on the phone with Bobby.

"Nah, they didn't say nothing after they went through the car. Indie didn't put up no fight he just went with them."

Ajai and Taj looked at each other before hopping off the stools and following Joey and Ricky down the hallway. "Where is Indie?"

"What is going on?" Ajai asked blinking her eyes quickly to focus on Ricky punching in the code to the safe.

Ajai watched as Joey paced on the phone and Ricky fidgeted with the safe. She watched as Taj bolted from the hallway to the front door to see Indie's car but no sign of him. "One of y'all got to tell us something."

Joey stopped mid pace to look at Ajai and Taj. "Indie is in jail."

Taj

HER HEART STOPPED. Her breathing hitched as she looked at Joey look back at her. Ricky got what he needed from the safe and closed it back. "What did you say?" her voice was small but everyone heard her.

Joey looked at Ricky, who looked back at him. Neither of them wanted to get her worked up because they knew that they could have him out in a matter of hours. "Somebody say something to me...why is he in jail? What happened? Is he okay?"

Joey locked eyes with Taj. "Cops arrested him... open container, weed, money and a gun..."

"Whose gun?" Taj questioned breaking eye contact with Joey to look at Ricky. "Yours? His hasn't left the glove box."

Ricky saw the flash of disappointment in Taj's eyes. She spun around in search of her shoes and her purse. "I'm going down there too."

"No, you're not, Baby," Joey spoke up taking a few strides to get to her and grabbed her by the arm. "You're drunk and it's nothing we can't handle."

"Really? Because this wouldn't have happened if it were

handled," Taj fussed at them. "This is the second time he's gotten pulled over in two days, for what?"

"Baby, just listen," Ricky spoke up, stepping to her. "We got it. We should be coming home with him. Just chill out okay?"

Taj looked up at Ricky with tears cradling her eyes because her mind was starting to run wild with the what if's. "Baby... breathe. It'll be okay. Aight?"

Taj quickly nodded her head and wiped her eyes. "Please call me with an update."

"We got you," Joey replied before walking out of the house and resuming his phone call with Bobby.

Ricky turned around and gave Ajai instructions. "Keep her calm, keep her in the house, and keep your phone on you."

"Okay," Ajai spoke softly. "I will."

With that Ricky left the house and closed the door behind him leaving Taj and Ajai standing there. Taj stared at the door and felt a wave of emotion take over her. Her chest was tight and she was trying to calm her racing mind but nothing she focused on was calming her. Ajai shuffled back into the kitchen and poured Taj a shot.

"I can't lose him again," Taj whispered to herself. Feeling Ajai's hand on her back, Taj turned around and took the shot from her hand and took it to the head. "What if they don't let him go that easy?"

"Then Bobby will do what he needs to get him out okay? Let's just relax and wait for them to call," Ajai suggested pulling Taj away from the door.

She couldn't help but feel like this was a repeat of that night all over again. Reluctantly being pulled away from the door so she wouldn't break down because she was close to it.

The shot of vodka didn't relax Taj a bit. She felt out of control while she was trying her best to control herself and not leave the house. Almost an hour had passed and Ajai lost her fight with sleep. Taj paced the floor with her phone and Ajai's phone in her hand waiting on something. The buildup of hearing about Indie was making her even more anxious than she already was. She thought that maybe if Indie had filled her in before she would have felt calmer with the situation. But because she didn't know anything every thought was running through her head.

After another forty-five minutes of pacing the hallway, the driveway and his bedroom, Ricky called Ajai. Taj quickly answered and pressed it to her ear. "Is he okay?"

Ricky released a sigh. "We can't bail him out tonight, Baby."

"Why not?"

"There is no bond set until he sees a judge. The judge is on vacation so who knows when that will be," Ricky replied.

That answer didn't satisfy Taj. She unlocked her phone and hailed an Uber. "Did you at least see him?"

"No," Ricky answered with a heavy sigh. "Hopefully tomorrow."

"Yeah, alright," Taj replied before hanging up on him. She grabbed one of Indie's hoodies to combat the California fall air that was starting to take over and her purse. The second the Uber pulled up she hopped in and anxiously bounced her leg until she got to the county jail. Before she climbed out, she looked at the driver and said. "Just wait on me...I'll be right back."

"Twenty minutes is all I can do," the driver responded.

She nodded her head and headed inside of the building. She looked around the empty lobby and waited at the counter for anyone to come and tend to her. It was almost ten minutes before an officer walked back around with a cup of coffee in his hand.

"Yeah, what can I do for you?" the officer didn't even look

at her. He was more concerned with whatever he was doing on his phone.

"Indigo Sims...I need to see him," she spoke up.

"Are you his lawyer?"

"No."

"Then I'm going to tell you like I told the other two, you have to wait until the judge gets back."

"I'm not leaving until I see him," Taj replied standing her ground hoping that it would get her what she wanted and that was to lay her eyes on Indie.

The officer chuckled and glanced up at her. "Would you leave if I told you that he wasn't here?"

Taj's head tilted to the side and her eyes squinted. "What I know is that he better be here. That's what I know. I know you guys have a tendency of losing black men but I won't let it happen. Lose everyone else's but mine."

She was trying her best to control her emotions but they were getting the best of her. "I've already lost him once; I cannot lose him again. Please just let me see him. I just need to make sure he's okay. Please...please."

The officer fully looked at her and couldn't deny her. The tears that welled up in her eyes made him want to give in. He looked around at the empty building and grabbed a ring of keys. "Five minutes is all I can do."

"That's more than enough," Taj muttered. "That's all I need."

Leading her back to the holding cells, Taj examined the empty cells looking for Indie. She finally spotted him at the end of the row, lying on the cot. "Baby!" Her heart dropped as she lightly jogged down to the end of the row. "Are you okay?"

"What are you doing here, Baby?" Indie shot up to his feet and leaped to the steel bars separating them.

Taj looked at this face and the tears that she was trying to hold spilled over. Indie had a cut under his eye and dry blood on his lip, the sight of him set her off even more. "What happened to his face? Did you do this? I swear if you did that's your fucking badge. He didn't leave the house like this!"

The officer shook his head and tapped his watch. Taj growled lowly and looked back at Indie. "Are you okay? Who did this to you?"

She reached through the bars and softly touched the cut under his eye making him wince slightly. "Tell me something, Indie."

Indie dropped his head and moved Taj's hand. With a kiss to her palm, he groaned, not wanting to tell her anything but he knew that she needed to know everything. "Promise me you'll wait until I get out to go back."

"I'm not leaving until you come home, but..."

"But I love you Taj. And I'm not leaving you again. I told you that. Whatever you want to know, I'll tell you when I get home okay?" Indie reached out to lightly brush his thumb over her lips. "I need you calm. Nothing else is going to happen to me okay? I'm always coming back for you baby."

Taj squeezed the tears from her eyes and looked back up at Indie. "You promise?"

"I promise. I won't put you through this shit again. Aight?"

"Okay. I love you, Indie."

"I love you. Get out of here. I'll call you in the morning to check on you."

Taj nodded her head and touched his face once more. "I'll keep your side warm."

"I'll be back in it before you know it."

"Alright, times up. Come on," the officers voice echoed down the row of cells.

Taj pulled herself away from the cell and slowly walked away from him. She glanced over her shoulder to see him watching her until she disappeared from his vantage point. Once she was back in the lobby, she wiped the residue of tears from her eyes and thanked the officer for his kindness. The Uber was still outside waiting on her, pulling the door open she glanced over at the driver and mumbled, "Thank you."

Arriving back home, she kicked her shoes off by the door, secured it and traveled back down the hall to his room. Ridding herself of her leggings she crawled into his side of the bed and inhaled his scent off the pillow. Squeezing the remaining tears from her ducts, Taj whispered a silent prayer before drifting off to a restless sleep.

CHAPTER TEN

*I*ndigo

Indie sat on the cot in the holding cell and scratched his overgrown facial hair. "I'm about sick of this shit."

He licked his dry lips, sat back, leaned his back against the wall, and shut his eyes. Sleep had been terrible, the food was worse, and being in isolation wasn't for him. Drumming his fingers against the wool blanket, he thought about everything else but his current situation.

Almost an hour went by before the heavy doors opened and feet shuffled in. He assumed it was another inmate waiting to be transferred over to the jail a few miles away or someone waiting for bail. Indie inhaled and heard the feet stop at his cell. Cracking an eye open, he looked over to see Bobby. Bobby's face was red, his lips were pursed together making the rest of his face twisted with angst. His tie was undone and he held his suit jacket in his hand along with his briefcase. Whatever happened before Bobby got here was intense enough for him to look so disheveled.

"Let's go home," Bobby's voice rumbled examining Indie's current state. "You good?"

"Besides wanting a shower and some food, I'm cool," Indie's voice was low being that he hadn't talked in three days to anyone. The last conversation he had was with Taj the first night he arrived. The continuation of that conversation he tried to push to the back of his mind so he didn't have to think about it. At least not until he got out.

Bobby stepped back and let the officer open the door. It was the same officer from the other night that let Taj back. Indie nodded at him and attempted to step around him but he blocked the way. "That girl you got...she's special. Don't come back here."

Indie nodded and said, "Appreciate it."

Bobby didn't utter another word until they were out of the building heading to his car. "I fucking swear. Holding you in that dirty ass cell for three days with no phone calls, no change of clothes and no hearing has me ready to set the damn building on fire. You know what they told me when I walked in there? That they couldn't find you ... they didn't even book you in."

Bobby's outward anger toward everything that happened was Indie's inside anger. "All they want is to make me talk about TK. I ain't doing that shit."

Bobby unlocked the car and directed Indie to get in. Doing so, Indie sunk his tired body into the plush leather seats. Bobby closed his door and started off down the street. "I would have been here a lot earlier but I had to go find the judge that was on vacation. Lucky for you, she's a good friend of mine and I told her about the constant run in's and the issues surrounding TK. Come to find out he was feeding the feds information about some people in your gang."

"Of course he was," Indie scoffed, narrowed his eyes and

looked out the window. "Was my name on anything that that nigga told?"

"No," Bobby shared. "Not yours, not Joey's, not Ricky's. I guess they thought if they applied pressure to you, that you would give them the missing key. But because they handled this entire case poorly, it was dismissed. You and your entire crew are off the hook. So, keep your nose clean. Pour every second of your time into your legitimate businesses and you'll be set, your family will be set, and I can transition from being your criminal lawyer to looking over contracts for you. You're a special man Indie. Very special."

"I appreciate that, Bobby. I really do."

"Show me by staying out trouble, alright?"

"You got it."

Indie got home and Taj pulled the door open before he could close the car door completely. She leapt for the threshold and wrapped her hands around his neck.

"You must have missed me?" Indie held her securely as he traveled into the house and shut the door.

Taj stood on her tip toes and held his face in her hands. She kissed his face repeatedly before replying, "I did. Are you okay?"

Her face was full of worry, her eyes were tired with red rings around them. "I'm home. I'm cool. Can your man get some food though?"

"Your mom made something earlier before she left," Taj replied trailing her hands from his face to his chest. "I'll warm it up. Go take a shower and relax."

Indie was expecting Taj to drill him with a million questions but instead she put her need to know to the back burner and put his need for comfort in front of whatever she wanted. She pulled herself away and walked into the kitchen and started warming food up for him.

Entering his bathroom, Indie peeled his clothes off, stuffed them into the laundry basket and hopped into the shower. Not caring about the temperature, he was happy that he could finally wash and lay in his own bed. Scrubbing the three-day jail funk off of him, he shut his eyes and made the decision to never turn back to old life. It didn't matter how tempting it was. Dealing, going on missions, fighting and begging his family to get right was behind him. They were all men and they all had responsibilities. Indie's responsibility was himself and his woman, nothing else would deter that. The chapter was closed, finally.

Once he showered and ate, he found himself sitting between Taj's thighs at the end of the bed. Indie's head laid on her left thigh, his arms wrapped around it while her right leg was draped over his shoulder. Taj's fingers were coated in coconut oil and massaged his scalp. He basked in the moment enjoying Taj serve him. He placed a kiss on her inner thigh and released a sigh.

Taj's voice was soft and soothing. "What's on your mind?"

"Nothing at the moment. I got a damn headache," he muttered. Without missing a beat, Taj popped up and scurried over to her bag, grabbed a tiny vile of oil, and returned to the bed taking her former position. She carefully dapped a tiny amount of oil on her fingertips and put the top back on it. Placing her fingers on his temples, Taj massaged the oil softly. Indie's shoulders relaxed and his head fell back deeper in her lap.

His eyes closely opened and locked with her large brown eyes looking back at him. "What are you doing to me girl?"

She chuckled softly and said, "Taking care of you. Rosemary is good for headaches. A trick I picked up from my mom."

"That's good shit," he hummed relaxing more. "If only she taught you how to cook."

"You got jokes like I won't wrap my legs around you and smother you." She giggled not taking her eyes off of his.

He smiled and licked his lips. "I'll eat my way out."

"Stop! You're nasty."

"You like it," he rumbled taking in a deep breath.

Taj hummed and moved her hands from his temples back to his scalp. "You be knowin'. Now tell me what's on your mind."

Indie swallowed and traced his fingers along her leg. "I'm at a point where I can't carry everything and everyone anymore...I'm over getting locked up over bullshit. Don't get me wrong, I love them. Ricky and I have been to war together and with each other but I'm getting too old for this shit. I earned my stripes, I did what I was supposed to do for him, for the set, for my hood. I want to live my life and not worry about what's around the next corner."

Taj's hands rested on the side of his face now, eyes still connected. He had all of her attention. The connection they shared was beautiful, like one of those paintings that hung up in your grandmother's house celebrating black love. Indie sat between her thighs contently in a pair of boxer briefs and his bare tattooed and scarred chest. Taj gladly allowed him to rest his troubles in her lap. Her college tshirt hung off her shoulders and the boy shorts she wore hugged her hips enough for Indie to admire how sexy she was without trying. Her large hair fell over her face like a veil.

"You're not done yet, babe," Taj replied. "You were never meant to be regular. You got a whole hood watching you, looking to you for a way out. You can be tired; you can be over it but you can't stop being who you were meant to be. This is so much bigger than you."

"What else can I do?"

"Everything," she replied with a smile. "All those trap

houses, all those houses that have a for sale sign hanging in front of them. Buy them. Flip them and sell them back to them. Put Joey over property management. Hire the kids to maintain the landscape. Show them another way besides hustling. Teach them ownership."

Indie's glare grew softer the more Taj spoke life back into him. "You can do whatever, but what you do has to have a purpose. Whatever you do has to be connected to who you are and what you are, baby. You got moves to make. I'll be right here every step of the way. Life is a marathon Indie. The reward isn't given to the fastest runner...but the one who endures. You got this babe."

Taj leaned further down to kiss his lips. Tenderly, slowly, and purposely making her intention with his heart clear. Indie couldn't deny the feeling that Taj's security provoked through his being. He knew without a doubt that he was her protection but Taj proved to be his too.

"You love a nigga huh?" he smirked softly against her lips before sitting up to get a full look at her.

Taj smiled warmly and moved upward to lay her head on the pillows. "Since the second you looked at me."

"Stop lying," he rumbled climbing into the bed with her. Pulling her closer to him, he wrapped his arms around her and Taj kissed the scar above his heart.

"I tell no lies," she crooned closing her eyes and throwing her leg over him.

"You should think about expanding your business too. Plus having you back in L.A. would be love."

"It would...you sure you're ready for me to have full access to you?"

Indie's chest vibrated with laughter. "I've been ready, Baby. I got my hooks in you now, I'm not letting go."

Taj yawned. "Please don't."

Taj drifted off to sleep, leave Indie lying there awake to think about what she said. She was right and he had to keep pushing even though he was tired. He knew that with Taj by his side he could do whatever he put his mind to because that was the energy she gave him. The feeling she enticed. She was strong enough to make him stop but soft enough to still make him feel like he was on top of the world. He needed her. He realized that years ago. But know he knew without a doubt that living life without her was out of the question. He planted his spirit inside of her and gave it to her so she could nurture it. It was the most selfless thing he'd ever experienced. Taj was the most beautiful spirit, the brightest light, the warmest set of arms he'd ever found.

CHAPTER ELEVEN

*T*aj

She looked at her bags on the floor and dreaded the idea of packing them with her stuff. She didn't want to leave Indie but she had pressing business she needed to get back to. She made a mental note to get Maria something nice for holding down everything while she was gone. Taj sat in the middle of her freshly washed clothes and pushed her hair out of her face. Her flight left in the morning and all she wanted to do tonight was wrap herself around Indie and hold him until it was time for her to leave.

"Get it together, Taj," she hummed to herself as she folded her clothes and packed them into their bags. She sat with her body facing the view of the ocean. That was her favorite part about this house outside of Indie himself. Taj loved everything about the ocean. It calmed her and turned her on at the same time.

She closed her eyes for a brief moment and thought about the first time she sat by the ocean with Indie. The way the moon shined down on them illuminated the aura that engulfed them. The feel of his lips on hers as he took control of her but he was gentle. He was always so gentle even when she was being difficult. Reminiscing the feeling of her flesh wrapped around his, they created a high that they kept chasing.

Hearing her alarm go off on her phone, she opened her eyes and released a huff of air. "I know, I know. Time for the stupid ass pill."

Taj pushed herself off the floor and walked into the bathroom to retrieve her pill case from her toiletry bag. "Where is it?"

Sifting through her things and growing aggravated that she couldn't find it, she dumped the contents across the counter and rummaged through it to find what she was looking for. And nothing. From the counter, she went through the trash and nothing. From the small trash can to her purse it was no luck. Plowing her fingers through her hair and scratching her scalp she groaned just as Indie walked into the room with a few bags in his hand.

"Woah, hurricane Taj." Indie whistled looking around the room. "You good?"

Taj squinted her eyes and pursed her lips out. She looked at him and shook the thought away. "Yeah, I'm good. I was trying to pack and them my alarm went off and I started looking for my pills. You haven't seen them, have you?"

A sly smirk crossed Indie's face. Taj mirrored his expression and tapped her index finger on her chin. "Did you throw them away?"

"How mad would you be if I said yes?" he questioned.

Taj pressed her tongue against the inside of her cheek and looked him behind the eyelashes. "If this were under any other circumstances, I would be pissed off. But because I know what I know, I'm cool with it."

"And what do you know?"

"Where you live in case you knock me up and ghost me," Taj joked starting to clean up her mess.

Indie laughed in relief and followed her into the bathroom and leaned on the wall. "You really think that?"

"Nah," she replied looking at him in the mirror. "I know that everything you do is intentional."

"And everything you do is logical. You take steps to make sure you don't end up in situations you can't get yourself out of." He paused and took a step toward her and placed his hands on her hips. Leaning down to kiss the curve of her neck. "You don't have to do that shit no more though."

Taj let her tongue trace her lips while she looked at him in the mirror. The security Indie gave her was far more invasive than the surface. He protected her from herself, her inner thoughts and her fear of failure. "You know sometimes, I think you're too good to be true."

Indie chuckled against her skin and kissed her neck again. It was just enough to make the hairs on the back of her neck stand up. "You haven't heard baby? I'm an urban legend."

Taj threw her head back into his chest and laughed with a snort. "You are annoying."

"I do my job, though. Come here. I got you something." Taking a few steps backward, Indie pulled her out the bathroom back into the room. Redirecting her attention to the bags on the bed he let her go. "Open them."

"Indie," Taj began to fuss but he cut her off with a kiss and a stern look to make her stop.

"I know what you can do for yourself. I know you don't need shit but me. But I wanted to do this for you. Open it up, get dressed, worry about packing in the morning and meet me downstairs. We got dinner reservations." Indie kissed her lips once more. "And Joey is at ma's for the night so..."

He flashed another sly smirk her way. "Don't keep me waiting too long."

"Okay."

Indie pulled the door closed behind him and left her there to pull the two boxes out of the bags. One box was a pair of black thigh highs and the other was a simple black dress. Both items that she specifically pointed out to Maria. "Oh, she wants a bonus."

Straightening up the room and freshening up, she applied a light layer of makeup and got dressed. She looked at herself in the mirror and started out the room. Stepping out the door, her black leather thigh highs were graced by red rose petals sprinkled over the hardwood. Pillar candles lined the hallway all the way out to the back porch where Indie was leaned over the railing with a glass of Hennessy in his hands and a blunt between his lips.

Taj stopped at the open glass door to admire him for a minute. She took a minute to thank God for him. All of those years of wanting him back. Needing him back and here he was. His shirt was unbuttoned and blowing in the wind. Taj got a glimpse of his tattoos and the scars she adored so much.

"What are you doing?" Taj asked with a giggle causing him to turn around.

"I'm out there trying to be fly and shit with my lady. You lookin' good Baby." Indie smirked, licked his lips and traced his eyes over her. "Turn around lemme see."

Taj flipped her hair over her shoulder and spun around slowly for him. "You like?"

"Hell yeah," he cheered. "Get over here."

Taj smirked his smirk and looked deep into his eyes as she strutted over making sure she built up his anticipation to feel her body on his. Wrapping her arms around his waist she kissed his bare chest and then looked up at him. "You smell good."

It was something about the smell of his woodsy cologne and his natural scent mixed with the smell of the OG Kush he smoked on the regular. It hypnotized her every time she inhaled it into her senses.

"You smell better."

"What's all this for?"

Indie tenderly kissed her lips and gripped her ass and followed it with a light smack making her ass cheeks ripple like a wave. "For you. Show my appreciation for you. I know this is where you want to be but sometimes life with a dangerous nigga is more than people bargain for."

"I knew what I was getting myself into. I wouldn't be here if I wasn't planning on being ten toes down."

She removed the glass from his hand and took the contents to the head. "Slow your ass down. Last time you did that, you gave me that pussy in the back seat of my Lincoln."

Taj bit her lips and grunted. "I'd do it again. There is no shame in my game, babe. You should feed me."

The drone of Taj's voice caused Indie's dick to brick up. His eyes got low as he watched her strut her sexy ass over to the table set for two. When she told him to feed her, it was a double meaning that he caught on to. He was going to need all his energy to deal with her freaky ass. When Taj got to drinking, she turned into an animal and was willing to put on a show for him. Anywhere and anytime.

"Maria wants a raise," Taj looked around the table at the champagne in the bucket, the candles and the vases of red and blue roses.

"Make sure you give it to her too. She came in with the clutch," Indie shared taking the cover off her plate.

"And prime rib... okay. You want it dirty tonight I see." She nodded her head. "Let's eat up."

"Why you so nasty, Baby?" Indie questioned in a low voice,

blowing smoke out his nose. "Hmm? Why do you do that to me? Knowing that there is nothing more I want than to be face down in your shit while you scream my name and push me deeper in the gushy."

Taj cut into her prime rib and flashed him a seductive look. "You make me comfortable. To be sexy as fuck, nerdy as fuck, relaxed as fuck. My brother used to tell me that these niggas out here are going to try you for clout. Just to say they fucked with you and leave. That they want what I can give them but not who I am. But you... you a different type of nigga."

"You right." Indie nodded his head with a cocky smirk. "I'm glad you know that shit."

"You know that I'm a different type of woman and you handle that shit accordingly. I'll be as nasty as you want wherever you want." After that statement she started eating her food leaving Indie to squirm in his seat and adjust himself.

As the night went on with shit talking, sexy glances exchanged, shots, and champagne, Taj was drunk and any inhibitions she had was gone with the breeze of the ocean a few hundred feet away. The staff Maria hired for the night cleared the table of the main course and left the dessert. Indie tipped them and requested they came back tomorrow to take care of everything else. Once they were out of sight, Taj reached under the table and wiggled herself out of her blue lace panties and handed them over to Indie.

He chuckled. "These are my favorite."

"I know, I didn't want you to tear them up. Keep those until I get back," Taj replied picking up her slice of chocolate cake and walking over to him with a hiked dress. "Sit back."

Indie did as he was told and welcomed Taj's straddle. His hands automatically pushed up her dress around her waist so her bare ass was out in the open.

Taj picked up a fork off the table and cut into the slice of cake. "Open up."

He did, taking the cake off the fork and licking his lips. "That shit is good. You know what will go good with that?"

"Tell me."

Indie swallowed, placed his middle finger in her mouth and let her suck on it before pulling it out and inserting it into her melting center. Her head dropped back and she chuckled in pleasure. Just as she began to rotate her hips around his finger, he pulled it loose, dipped it into the frosting on the cake and sucked it off his finger. "Got damn that shit is good."

"I know." She put the plate down, pushed his shirt off his shoulders and kissed his lips so she could taste herself on his tongue. Taj moaned, getting more aroused by the brush of her tongue against his.

Indigo pushed her dress of her shoulders exposing her breasts to the night air. Firmly wrapping his arms around her waist, he stood up and laid her on the table. Rubbing his hands over her soft thighs he moaned with pleasure at the sight of her flower under the candlelight. He was thankful that the table was big enough to fuck around and tear up the porch.

Taj loved the low lustful look in his eyes as he ran his hands over her body. "Eat your cake, baby."

"Don't rush me, Baby. I'll eat when I'm fuckin' ready," he grunted pushing a finger inside of her folds. Her juices spilled over making him chuckle at the sight of her face of pleasure. "You know you're a fuckin' drug."

"I know," she moaned. "Better than any weed you ever smoked."

Twirling his finger around he pulled it out placed in her mouth and bent over to devour her. Her back arched on contact, she sucked her juices from his finger and moaned. The sensation of his tongue running over her folds was replaced by hard dick without warning making her cry out into the night. "Oh fuck!"

Indie's breathing got heavy as he pumped without mercy holding her legs up on his shoulders. "Got damn, Baby."

His pumps got more intense and she knew that he was on the edge of his first explosion. Regaining control, she pushed him out and hopped off the table and squatted down. Grabbing him and taking him into her mouth whole, she sucked her juices off and moaned when his hands found the root of her hair. With her hands resting on her knees, Taj sucked him until his seeds shot down her throat and he loudly groaned into the night.

He pulled her up to face him. "Go to the room and stand in the window, just like that. I want to see that ass walk away."

She licked her lips, grabbed her breasts roughly and walked away from him. Slowly... so he could enjoy the view. Once she got inside the house, she bent over to adjust her thigh high boots and continued to the room. Entering the room and standing in the window she noticed a few people strolling the beach. For a second she came back to her senses, but then Indie wrapped his arms around her body. His dick was back at attention and pressed against her back and his lips found her neck. He ran a hand down the front of her body and began to play with her pearl.

"That shit is wet as fuck," he mumbled against her skin. "Prop your leg up."

Taj propped her leg up in the window seal and rested her head on his shoulder. "There's people watching us."

"Fuck them niggas, take this dick and give them a show." His breathing got heavy as he positioned himself at her opening from the back.

"Feed me, Indie."

"Say it again," he commanded pushing into her ocean.

"Ah, feed me," she buzzed feeling all of him spread her open. "Just like that."

"I got it from here, hold on to me tight."

CHAPTER TWELVE

*I*ndigo

The length of Taj's hair fell over his shoulder and covered his chest as she laid her head on his chest and her body wrapped around him. Indie wiped the sleep from his eyes and looked around the room. Handprints in the window, towels on the floor, sheets scattered about were all signs that the night before was lit. They made sure they gave each other enough love to last them for a week until she returned back to him.

She stirred a little as he ran his hands through her hair and kissed the top of her head. "Wake up baby. You got to pack."

"Mm mm," she groaned rolling over and poking her ass out. He chuckled running his hand over her bare body. "I don't want to leave."

"I'll fly in a few days after the walk through," he assured her scooting behind her and wrapping his arms around her waist. "You want breakfast?"

"I just want to lie here a little while longer. I feel like I ran a marathon."

"Shit, we did. You see what this room looks like?"

Taj chuckled softly and said, "I don't want to open my eyes and find out."

"I'm going to miss you," he replied after kissing her bare shoulder. The crook of her neck, the curve of her jaw, and behind her ear.

"I'm going to miss you." Taj rolled over to face him and draped her leg over his waist. "This house... a couple of days seems so long."

Indie couldn't help but grip her ass and run his fingers don't the crack of her ass to the opening of her flower. "Why are you wet like this already?"

She stretched and laughed, then ran her fingers along his body. "You just do something to me. I crave you all the time."

"Oh yeah?"

"Mhmm," she rolled locking eyes with him. "Can I just leave my things here and not pack them?"

"Of course," he whispered fingering her until he was fully at attention. "I bought this house for you...for us."

"You knew I was coming back... didn't you?"

"Sho did. You got my heart in your hands, I wasn't letting you walk away with it," he answered, putting his finger in her mouth and slowly pushing his dick inside of her with a low heavy groan. Holding her close to him he pumped in and out hitting her spot and watching her eyes puddle with tears. "You know I love you."

That did it, the tears streamed down her face while she took all of him. He felt her body quiver and shake under him. He watched her hold her gaze and her breath. "Breathe, Baby."

"Ohhhhh," she released followed by an 'ahhhh'. "I love you, too. I missed you so much. This dick. Those eyes. These lips. That heart."

Every word that followed from her lips was drenched with euphoria. "All of you."

Indie clamped down on his lip and continued to deliver the deep slow strokes that had her unraveling and soaking his thighs and the sheets. Kissing her deeply, his moans got a little louder when she hummed, "I'm cumming. Give me everything."

He did, unloading all of his milk into her river and panted into the curve of her neck. Their session was so passionate that they both fell back asleep and were woken up by the blaring of her alarm indicating that they only had an hour to beat L.A. traffic and get her on her flight.

Taj shot up and ran to the bathroom to jump in the shower and he was right behind her. "Go stand on your side. I'm going to end up fucking you again and missing my flight."

Indie chuckled and went to the other side of the shower and washed off. He made sure to keep his body turned to the wall so he wouldn't be tempted to connect with her again.

They showered, dried off and rushed to get dressed. "Don't worry about the mess, I'll take care of it. Grab your purse and your phone."

She slipped her feet into a pair of sneakers and grabbed his hoodie. "Come on, I'm ready."

They rushed out the house, hopped in the car and sped towards the airport. "Fucking with you is dangerous, I swear. I'm so happy I own this company." Taj's laugh filled the car as she applied lotion to the parts of her body that were exposed.

"I was never safe."

"Never. I should have known you were trouble."

"Good trouble. That nigga that'll fight for you and have your body creaming on command."

"I see no lie," she hummed. "That's why I fuck with you. You can handle me."

"I can't wait to handle you again. When you get there make sure you call me."

"You already know that," Taj commented. "Two days."

Reaching the airport, he parked the car and walked inside to the terminal with her. Holding her hand and checking his text, he tried to distract himself from getting emotional at her departure. He was always emotional about leaving her. That's what made being in love with her dangerous. Nigga's could use that shit against him, but he knew that Taj could hold her own too. No one was getting an upper hand on either of them. They were lethal together and that's what he loved.

"Now boarding business class rows A-C to San Francisco." The announcement was made and Taj sighed heavily before standing up.

Indie stood up and took her face into his hands and kissed it. "Call me when you get there. If anything pops off make sure I'm the first call. "

"I will. I love you, stay safe."

"Stay dangerous, Baby."

With that he released her and put his hands in his pockets watching as she walked away.

Taj

"Oh, perfect they changed the locks," she hummed punching the code Maria texted her in the door. Taj walked into her condo and looked around. Nothing about it felt comfortable anymore. All the traces of Malcolm had been removed which she was happy about but nothing here represented how she felt now. The walls were dark, reminding her of the pain she was carrying when she had them painted.

Walking into her room she removed her clothes applied lotion to her body and pulled out a pink dress and pulled it over her body. Taj placed a pair of hoops in her ears and her watch on her wrist. She shot Maria a quick text telling her that she'd be in the office in twenty and slipped her feet into a pair of nude pumps. Taj gathered her things she before walking out the condo and made her way to the parking garage.

Once she was in her car and headed toward the office, she called Indie. He must've been waiting on her call because he answered on the second ring. "You good, Baby?"

"I'm good. I'm on my way to the office. I might be there all night. We have investments and a strategy meeting plus I have to dive into everything I missed."

"I need to get you a gun or something," he replied with a sense of uneasiness. "I don't like you being away from me."

"I don't like being away from you but this is how it's going to be for a minute. Back and forth." She pouted a bit.

"Nah, not for long. Focus on the road and call me when you leave. Make sure security walks you to your car. If that bitch pops up, I want to know."

"I hear you, Daddy."

"I'm not playing with you girl. I'm dead ass serious."

"I know you are. I'll call you I promise," she said in a sing a long voice. "Miss you already."

"Me too, but you got a bag to get and I'm not standing in the way of that shit. Go kill em, killa."

Taj chuckled and they exchanged another set of I love you's and call you soon's. She hung up and pushed on to her office. Getting to the office she was greeted with a big hug and squeal. "I missed you so much."

Taj smiled big and hugged her back. "I missed you too. You kept everything intact. I'm proud of you."

She released her and walked into her office only to see a vase of flowers on her desk and a teddy bear that had "Miss You

Already" stitched on its shirt. Taj's smile widened so much that her wide eyes disappeared behind her rosy cheeks.

Maria closed the door and sat down. "Soooo, tell me about your vacation. You are glowing girl!"

"First of all," Taj started after smelling the flowers and hugging her bear like a teenager. She sat in her seat slowly still sore from all the attention Indie had given her body. "You deserve a raise so expect that. Second of all, it was fucking beautiful. Minus all the bullshit that occurred. I am beyond happy."

"You deserve it," Maria swooned over Taj's bright smile and new outlook on life. "Aren't you happy I made you go back?"

"Yes, I am. How are you and your beaux? You are glowing too."

Maria blushed just as much as Taj did. "So, he gave me the key to his place. We're discussing moving in together."

"That's amazing. You deserve to be happy...and ironically enough," Taj stopped and looked at Maria's smile. "I'm thinking about expanding."

"Oh really?"

"Really and I need something to run this office," Taj announced.

Maria quickly entered back into work mode and started rambling off questions. "How many applicants do you want to see? Any particular credentials? And preference?"

Taj laughed and leaned up on her desk and looked at Maria. "I want you."

"Excuse me?" Maria's face twisted.

"I want you to run it. You know the in's and out's, you have been here since the beginning and you deserve it. I didn't build this alone; you were right there. Since high school. Why would I overlook you Maria?"

Maria covered her mouth and tears formed in her eyes. "Don't play with me."

"I'm not playing. You are my best friend. My only friend. You deserve the world. If I can share a piece with you, I will. You will be promoted in a few weeks. When I go back to L.A. I'm going to find an office space."

Maria sat back in disbelief and looked at Taj. "How is it that everything we dreamed is coming to fruition?"

"Because God is good." Taj's answer was simple but powerful enough to make her stop. "For so long I was angry at Him because of everything we had to go through to get here. But without any of that we wouldn't be here. My beef with Him is over. He has proven Himself to me time after time. You deserve this."

"And so do you."

Maria and Taj stood up to embrace each other. Tears fell from their eyes as they held on to one another. "Ride or die."

"Bonnie and Clyde." Taj laughed through the tears. "I love you so much."

"I love you too best friend. Always and forever."

They pulled away from each other and Taj sat on the edge of her desk. "You're going to move to L.A. and start your life with the man you love. I'm starting my life with the man I love. You realize that we are grown as fuck now?"

"We sure are," Taj beamed. "This feels so surreal to me."

"Well pinch yourself you're not dreaming. This is real life, real love, and it's here right now."

Before Taj fixed her mouth to answer, Indie Facetime' d her. She answered and flashed the camera on Maria. "What's good, girl?"

"Hey Indie! How are you? You look rested."

"I am. Take care of my girl, I want her back soon."

"She's all yours," Maria shared with a smile. "I'm going to leave you two to it."

"See you soon!" Indie waved as Maria walked out the door.

Taj flipped the camera back around to her and smiled at him. "Thank you for my flowers and my bear. I'm going to sleep with that tonight."

"I was just calling to make sure you got them. I feel like I'm having withdrawals. When you moving in?" he questioned in a joking tone but Taj knew he was serious.

"Mmm, I'll let you know. How's the buildings?"

"Keeping playing, I'll kidnap your ass."

"No need I'll go willingly."

He smirked into the camera. "I know. Everything is good. Buildings are almost done and I found a two-story building for the STEM center. That's next on the list. Tomorrow I'm going to meet with a realtor."

"Look at you making waves like a player," Taj responded.

"Because I am. So, when are you moving in?"

"You are shameless."

Indie licked his lips and studied her. "You damn right."

"I'll start packing tonight."

"Just bring your clothes, you don't need nothing else."

Taj's dimples pierced her cheeks as she smiled like a schoolgirl. "Okay, I got to get to work. I love you. Go be productive."

"Aight."

CHAPTER THIRTEEN

*S*enior

"I am so happy we got to do this again." Maggie's eyes beamed across the table at Senior who faintly smiled back.

Senior noticed how easy for she took a liking to him. Through the course of their time together Maggie was sure to tell Senior that he was the type of man who held a mystery behind his dark eyes.

He was sure to keep the things that made him tick unknown, to everyone, including her. But he knew that she wanted to know. He sensed that Maggie wanted more than just his friendship. Considering it had been years since he had a woman in his life, he gave into Maggie easily.

She was beautiful. Even in her mid-fifties she still held her girlish figure and her sepia skin glowed. If he had to be honest with himself, he would admit that she made him stop in his tracks the first time he laid eyes on her. Senior was okay with being alone the rest of this life. He'd experienced the greatest of losses. And with his relationship with Taj on ice he was on the verge of another loss.

His strong, independent, and resilient daughter was no longer someone he could sway with the tone of his voice. Taj was now a grown woman, with grown needs and stubbornness unmatched for any of the tools he possessed. No matter how hard he tried, Senior couldn't accept being okay with the idea that Taj fell madly in love with a man like...him.

Indie reminded Senior of himself. A young wild nigga that was reckless and dangerous laced with good intent and a point to prove. From the second those two sparked, Senior knew that he was in for a fight to get his daughter to find someone not like...him.

Clearing his throat, Senior pulled himself out of his head and admired how Maggie's short black hair framed her face. It was a new haircut that he'd been complimenting for some days now. "I am too. I wasn't planning on storming out the last time but this is our redo."

"How is everything with Taj? I haven't seen her around," Maggie commented. "You miss her...I see it in those dark eyes of yours. You carry so much inside."

Senior sucked in a deep breath and picked up his glass. "I'm not sure how she's doing. I can only see how she's doing via Facebook and Instagram and since she's started her business, she hasn't really been on either. Her aunt gives me an update but it's nothing like seeing your child. I do miss her. But that girl is her own woman. The thing about Taj is that she'll hold on to a grudge until she's ready to let go of it."

"Charles," Maggie said before she chuckled lightly. "You're her father. She might not always like the things you do or even understand them. But *you're* her father. You're the one she will base every relationship off. I know I did. The first question I used to ask myself was, how does this guy compare to my father? Daughter's learn how to love from their father's. They are either looking for you or looking to appease you..."

Senior groaned and put his glass down. Maggie smirked. "From that reaction and what you've told me about her with Malcolm, she has done the latter. You need to repair that relationship before it isn't repairable."

"I hear you."

"Are you listening to me? I'm dropping free game," she joked holding her arms out to her side.

Senior chuckled softly, licked his lips and asked, "Do you continue to compare men to your father?" Maggie grinned and nodded. "How am I on that list?"

"I'll let you know when you take me home tonight," she replied holding her glass up.

The rest of the night had gone better than planned. Senior found himself putting his troubles with Taj to the side and enjoying Maggie's company fully. He walked her to the front door, cupped her face before she reached for her keys and kissed her supple lips. Maggie's cheeks flushed red and she bit her lip.

"I'll be seeing you soon?" she asked looked up at him with her wide hazel eyes that damn near made him putty in her hands.

He grinned and dropped his hands back to his sides. "Yes, you will. Take care. Stay safe."

"Always."

He waited until she was fully inside of the house before jogging down the steps and climbing back into his car. He had a few minutes to kill until he got home and he decided to call Taj.

The phone didn't even ring, it went straight to voicemail. Trying it again and again and again he got the same result. It infuriated him. He didn't know whether or not she was still in L.A. but either way he wanted to see her and plead his case.

Senior stewed in his aggravation until he got home and

tried calling her again. It was evident that Taj had blocked his number. The only person who knew how she was doing was someone he never wanted to have another conversation with.

Indie.

Indie held the key to Taj and that allowed him to have an upper hand over Senior. He hated it.

He sat on the couch and hoovered his finger over Indie's name. Senior had brought himself enough nerve to call and try to talk this feud out with Indie. Hitting his name, he put the phone on speaker and waited for him to answer.

The first time the phone rang until it went to voicemail. Instead of leaving a message, Senior called back. He had every intention to talk to Indie peacefully and respectfully.

After four rings, Indie answered. "Who this?"

"You know who this is," Senior grumbled into the phone losing all intent to have a pleasant conversation with him.

Indie grunted and then chuckled. "Charles Adams Senior. How can I help you today?"

Instantly Senior was pissed off by the arrogance in Indie's voice. "Where is my daughter?"

"Why didn't you call her if you wanted to know her location? Oh yeah, that's right. She ain't fucking with you right now."

"Listen you smug son of a bi—"

"Aht Aht," Indie warned. "Watch your mouth."

"You need to stay away from her. I've already told you once, twice and a third. Don't go for a fourth."

"My nigga. That sounds like a threat. I don't do threats old man. You want to talk to your daughter; you call your daughter. That's your problem to fix and it has nothing to do with me," Indie replied proudly. "Is that all?"

Senior scoffed. "Nah it ain't. Stay away from her."

Indie's hearty laugh filled Senior's living room. "Look my

G, something is wrong with you...that ain't ever going to fucking happen. But you be cool, stay safe. These streets are dangerous."

With that Indie hung up leaving Senior brewing with his face twisted. "Son of a bitch!"

Knocking the books off his coffee table, Senior became unhinged and shot to his feet and paced the floor. All the emotion that Senior had been holding inside started to seep out through the cracks of his foundation. The tears streamed from his eyes as he thought about his wife's unexpected death. He wasn't there to protect her. Then Bubba's death, he wasn't there to protect him or Taj. Bubba protected Taj, Bubba molded Taj, Bubba taught Taj the game. More than anything Senior was torn apart by guilt. The guilt of working immensely hard to provide his family a better life that they flashed before his eyes. Taj was all he had left. And if he had to humble himself and fess up to all of his sins against her to repair what he single handedly broke he would have to do it. Even if that meant starting with Indie and talking to him like the man he was.

DEVVON TERRELL: BORN SINNER

Protect me from my troubled past
Feel like the storm I'm in will never pass
Sometimes when I get happiness, man, it never last
I'm holdin' on, I'm really drowning tryna hit the surface
Looking at my sins like was it worth it?
No, this is fate
Night's I wasn't safe brought me to a better place
I'm a born sinner.

CHAPTER FOURTEEN

*R*icky

"This shit is looking good," Ricky cheered dapping hands with Joey. Joey's face flashed with a proud expression. "You got some finesse that I don't have. All that time I spent fighting with their asses to get this shit done."

Joey chuckled and headed out one of the suites and walked up toward the front of the building. "Finesse. It's a Sims thing. Yours skipped over a generation, maybe Bleu will have it."

"You and your brother like talking shit," Ricky scoffed before he popped the seal on his water. Walking out of the building he leaned on the hood of his car and looked around. Leroy was busy making sure the entire complex was clean. For a second Ricky felt guilty for not taking him seriously before. All he needed was someone to give him a chance.

Joey's low laugh took Ricky's attention off of Leroy and back on him. "Remember y'all used to get kicked out of here for playing your music too loud and selling your work?"

"Man, listen. Indie got arrested right over there for running his mouth to the cops." Ricky pointed over to the right where the corner was. "Now he owns this shit."

"Nah you got it wrong," Joey muttered looking over at Ricky. "We own this shit. There's never been nothing he set out on and didn't include us. I see that chip on your shoulder. Get rid of that shit. Ain't nobody looking at you differently. We know you're your own man with your own vision. So, what are you going to do about it?"

Ricky looked at the storefront that Indie handed over to him for him to do whatever he wanted to do with it. He hummed to himself and thought about the sketch books he hid under his bed. The only people who knew about it were Ajai and Indie. Since everyone was living their dream, he had to too.

Him and Joey exchanged a few more words as Indie pulled into the parking lot and parked his car by Ricky's. Indie killed the engine and hopped out. "What you niggas doing?"

"Shit," Joey started. "Nothing, looking through the buildings and double checking the list. Everything is move in ready."

"I like that." Indie nodded his head with a smile, dapping both of them up. "Y'all ate?"

"Nah not yet. What you got in there some Fat Burger?" Ricky asked with a chuckle. "Did you ever go back and quit?"

"No," Indie scrunched his face up before he laughed. "Fuck them. I hated that damn job."

The three of them laughed for a few seconds and Indie broke away. "Ay, follow me. Let me get Leroy."

"He didn't have to tell me twice," Joey mumbled. "I'm hungry as hell."

Ricky watched as Indie walked over to Leroy and convinced him to come along for the ride. "I know you hungry don't even tell me no, nigga. We going to break bread like family. Come on. Ain't nobody going to bother your stuff, they'll have to see me."

"Alright, Indie." Leroy shuffled behind him to Indie's car and climbed in.

About twenty minutes later they arrived at the restaurant and were sitting around the table cracking jokes. A feeling was taking over Ricky that he'd been trying to sort out for a while. It would come and go but today it was stronger than it had ever been.

"Leroy, you been doin' good!" Indie talked over the noise of the restaurant. "I'm proud of you for sticking to your word and showing up every day, on time, and you ain't been drinking either."

Leroy smiled and looked around the table. "Ah come on Indie. You know that ain't a problem man. You're family. You look out. It's the least I could for you."

"Nah, don't do it for me. Do it for you. Listen, I'm going to hire you permanently to maintain these buildings. I got you a place to stay, I got you some new clothes in my trunk just keep doing what you doing. Aight?" Indie looked at Leroy who had tears in his eyes from joy. Leroy wrapped his arm around Indie and patted his back. "If I got it you got it."

Indie and Leroy released each other and Indie looked at the three of them. "I mean that shit. We in this together. This is our shit. We hustled for it, we bled for it, we took losses for it and we're going to grow this shit from the ground up."

Ricky nodded his head and cleared his throat. "Since we having this moment, I just want to say I appreciate you. I know I've done some shit that was uncalled for but you stepped to me as a man and handled me like that. You sacrificed a lot for us and I know for me, I will never overlook that shit."

Indie stood up to bring Ricky into a half hug half hand shake. "You my brother. You my nigga. I wouldn't be shit without you. I love you."

"Same bro," Ricky shared feeling a weight fall off his shoulders.

After the moment passed and the food came to the table they talked about the tenants, the STEM program and the new houses that he was in the process of getting. "You look refreshed though."

"A young nigga is getting more than he can stand," Indie replied rubbing his chest with a lazy smile crossing his face. "Speaking of which. Senior called me last night."

Ricky groaned, rolled his eyes and fell back in his seat. "Fuck he want?"

"For him to be your fam you don't like that nigga too much." Joey snickered.

"Don't nobody like that nigga too much," Ricky scoffed. "He's that old mean ass uncle you stay away from."

"He wanted me to back up from Taj." Indie snickered with a look of disbelief.

Ricky and Joey started laughing.

"Tell him to go sit down," Joey commented and Ricky piggy backed the comment.

"In a corner. He trippin'. 'Cause if you back up off her Joey is goin' to shoot his shot and he still won't be able to get rid of you."

Indie

AFTER DROPPING Leroy off and getting him situated in his new home, Indie headed to check on his mom. He strolled into the house and found her on the couch with a magazine in her lap and the phone pressed to her ear. "Mary, the ghost of Christmas just walked in. I'll call you back...bye."

"What's up? What you doing today?" Indie asked kissing her cheek and taking a seat.

"What I'm doing right now. I don't have to chase you two around anymore now I can relax," Diane spoke up. "Although a little birdie told me that you had a nice stay in a cell for a few days."

Indie rolled his eyes and shook his head. "Who was the birdie? I know it wasn't Joey."

Indie watched his mother raise her brow and cut her eye at him. "Who do you think fed and calmed Taj down for three days? Poor girl was a mess. I hope that's the end of your foolishness. It's not just you anymore."

"Ma." Indie slouched in the seat and let an exasperated sigh push through his lips.

Diane snapped her head and looked at him fully. "Don't ma me, Indie. You're a grown ass man you can't do the shit you used to."

"You know I didn't come over here to hear you fuss at me." Indie looked up at the ceiling with his hands resting flat on his legs.

"Well... I'm not done. I need you to talk to Senior."

He laughed loudly and ran his hand down his face. "I'm not talking to that nigg- man about nothing. If he wants to talk to Baby, he can do that himself. I don't have shit to do with what he did."

"Do you know what he did?" Diane requested a response from Indie other than I don't know.

Indie frowned and shook his head no. "All I know is that he told that lame ass nigg- clown she was with he'd give him a share of her company if he married her. Anything else beyond that, I don't want to know about it because I'd really have to go have a conversation with him. I'm trying my best not to do that."

"Hm, well son, either way Senior only has one route to his daughter and that's through you. So, I need you to put your pride aside and handle that. Think about it, what if you were in his shoes?"

Indie wasn't here for the comparisons. "First of all, I wouldn't have done half the things that Senior has done to Baby to my seed. Who does that? And why are you taking up for him?"

"I'm not taking up for him. I'm speaking as a parent. Besides you, Baby's relationship with Senior is the most important relationship she could have. It needs to be repaired and although you don't want to be...you're the gatekeeper. You need to put your feelings to the side and take care of this."

"I hear you," he muttered not liking the idea at all but he knew it was going to boil down to this. Taj was just as stubborn as her father was. Indie had experienced it with his own eyes. If it hadn't been for divine intervention, he would have still been hunting her down.

"But are you listening?"

He huffed and cut his eyes at his mom quickly before she caught him. "I got it, Ma. Your wish is my command."

"I like to hear that." Diane smiled as Indie pushed himself up.

"Mm hm. You know Indo likes when the women in his life are happy," he replied stretching. "I'm going to head out."

"I'll see you soon."

Indie angled himself over his mother to kiss the top of her head. "Love you."

"Love you more. Be safe out there."

There was nothing more Indie hated right now than having to reach out to Senior and talk to him. In fact, he thought about every way to get out of it on his drive home but he could see his mother's scowl in the back of his head. "I really don't want to talk to this nigga, cuh."

He hit the phone icon on the screen of his car and hit Senior's number. As the phone trilled through the car, Indie curled his lip upward hoping that he wouldn't answer. "God, we don't talk often and that's on me. But please, don't let this nigga pick up."

Senior picked up and grumbled, "What do you want?"

"Aight, I see what You did," Indie grumbled to himself. "You want to talk to Baby or not?" Indie pushed back. "We meeting up or not 'cause I got shit to do."

"Where?" Senior grunted just as unwilling as Indie was to have this conversation.

"Tomorrow at noon, I'll text you the location."

CHAPTER FIFTEEN

*I*ndie

"Hey babe!" Taj beamed through the screen on the phone clutched in his hand. "When are you getting here?"

"In a couple hours. I need to tie up some shit before I fly up there and get lost in you," he responded looking at her adjust her shirt. "Don't cover them ant hills up now. You had them all on the counter, leave them there."

"You like these ant hills. Stop playing," Taj smacked her lips. "Anyway, I called because I got some good news for you."

"What's that? You're packed up and ready to bring your ass back down here where you belong?" Indie's sly smile made Taj roll her eyes. "Don't roll them pretty ass eyes at me, Baby. I'll make em roll for real."

"Anyway." She giggled and quickly collected herself. "Your investment was wired over this morning. Congratulations! I wanted to tell you myself."

Indie broke out in an uncontrollable grin. "Stop playing."

"No games. It's all you. That's your dream, babe." Taj's

face mirrored his joyous expression. "I'm proud of you. I can't wait to see what you do with it."

The loud roar of Senior's soaped up engine invaded Indie's ear drums and caused him to look over his shoulder then back at his screen. "Baby, I'll see you soon aight?"

Taj blew a kiss through the screen. "I love you."

"Love you."

Hanging up and sliding his phone into his pocket, he stood up from his seated position and waited for Senior to exit his car. When he did, Indie snarled a bit at the way Senior looked him up and down. "Traded in your khakis for a suit?"

"If you listened more than you ran your mouth you would know I'm legit now," Indie grumbled walking toward the door of his STEM center. The glass doors were covered by parchment paper to keep the people walking by from looking in. Opening the door, he held it so Senior could walk in. "This is Radius 180."

Senior fully walked into the open space and looked around in awe. Indie locked the doors and started walking around. He came to the conclusion that the best way to get Senior to see him as more than a thug was to show him his passion. "This is a safe, secure place for the neighborhood kids to come and learn about science, technology, engineering and mathematics. I've been saving up for this building for almost six years. Everything I did, everything I went through was to get to this point. I got a few other businesses but this is my pride."

Indie climbed the stairs to the loft and looked down at the concrete slab below. "I'm not just some nigga from the set your daughter fell in love with."

Senior scoffed and continued to look around. "Oh yeah? Did drug money pay for this?"

Indie chuckled softly and shook his head. "That's not the

point, Charles. The point is I made it out and I'm bringing a whole lot of niggas with me. Can you say you did that?"

He looked at Senior in the face and let a smug expression cross his and counter Senior's grim expression. "Hm cuh? 6oth street Chucky. I asked around about you..."

Senior swallowed the lump in his throat and avoided Indie's glare. "Nah, don't look away from me, cuh. Look at me in the damn face like a man. You got in some shit and ran when it got too hot and never looked back until you had to. Scared the fuck out of you didn't it?"

Indie's scowl intensified. Senior was no better than he was. The only difference in Indie's eyes was that he came back and faced his issues head on. "To bring your only child back here and she fall for a nigga just like you. It's not me... it's not me that you're fightin'. It's your fuckin' self. You don't have to say shit. I know. I see it. It makes sense now."

Senior flared his nostrils and looked away. He arched his body over to rest his elbows on the rail and look into the space around them. "We went on a mission. You know normal gang shit. They ran up on us so we went back to serve them. My cousin was driving... it was just supposed to be an in and out thing. But we were outnumbered. One thing led to another and they shot him point blank in the chest. That didn't kill him, though. The beating across the head with the crow bar over and over again was what did it. I watched him bleed out on the pavement. I stood there long enough to hear the sirens before I ran. I left him there. On the pavement dying."

Indie stared at Senior intently. Senior clenched his eyes shut. "I went home packed enough to travel with no issues. Took some cash and went to Virginia. That's where I met Taj's mother. She didn't care about who I was and what I did...or didn't do. She just loved me with all her heart. Just like Baby loves you. It's scary how much of her mother she actually is and doesn't know it. So anyway. My wife was killed by a drunk driver on her way home from work one night. I was supposed to drop her off and pick her up but I took on an extra shift. After her funeral, I packed Bubba and Taj up and moved them to North Carolina. Raised them the only way I knew how. Bubba started falling into my old footsteps and was killed for it. And I wasn't there, I was workin'. The night they drove by my sister's house in attempts to kill you I saw her life flash before my eyes. She's all I got left. Just her. I promised myself that I would never not be there to protect her again. And..."

Senior balled up his face and let a tear roll down his face. "What I thought was her protection was a bigger threat than you. Someone who wore sheep's clothing but when the doors closed, he put his hands on her, raped her and treated her with no regard toward the end."

Indie's blood began to boil. But he didn't react. He was too smooth for that. He would finish with Senior before he handled Malcolm accordingly.

"Indigo... I was wrong. I was wrong to keep her from you. I was wrong to give her over to that nigga for a price. I thought I was making the best decision for her but I see I fucked up and honestly I have no idea how to get this back on track."

Indie couldn't really be mad at Senior's lack of problem solving, he understood. This man lost almost everything he loved and was just trying his best to hold on to the last bit of his family. "It was so much easier to hate you...but I get it nigga. You were just out here trying to protect your baby. But I'm the last nigga out here that wants to hurt her. It killed me to be away from her that long. To watch her from afar go through the motions. If I could take it back I would. But I can't. I have to move forward. I got a second chance to do it. And you are on your tenth but hey."

Indie chuckled softly to loosen the thickness in the air. "All jokes aside. Had you led with that I wouldn't of gave you so much hell. Because I love your daughter and I want the best for her. I'll hook up a meeting. You need to step to her with the truth though. She's not a kid no more, she damn sure ain't that girl I met four years ago. Baby is a grown ass woman who found her voice and her strength when everything tried to break her. You need to go in this meeting with that in mind."

Senior stood up straight and held his hand out for a hand-shake. "Thank you."

"Ain't no need to thank me yet. She's stubborn as shit and both of us might be on ice depending on how this meeting goes. I'll bring her back here to talk to you."

"Thanks for looking out."

"It's not for you. It's for her. I'll do whatever I need to do to make sure she's good," Indie finalized.

With that, they wrapped up their meeting and went their separate ways. After locking up the building Indie climbed into his car and called his cousin.

"What's going on Indo!" his cousin Rodney shouted through the phone. "Heard you making waves down there."

"Ain't shit. I got some shit movin'. I need you though...you seen Bookie around? He not in jail?" Indie questioned with a scowl.

"Nah, that nigga just got out too. What's going on?"

"I need y'all niggas to be on standby, I'll be there in an hour or two."

"Aight, cuh. I got you."

Indie hung up and called Ricky, then Joey and sync'd their calls together. "We in 8th grade with this three-way call?" Ricky questioned.

Joey snickered. "Why are you frontin' like you made it to the 8th grade?"

"I did, Indie didn't. Anyway...what's up?" Ricky asked.

"Y'all might need to catch a quick flight. We need to pull up on a nigga." Indie's voice was low letting both Joey and Ricky know that shit was about to get real and quick.

Joey sounded off first. "Fuck is going on?"

"Ricky you know that nigga was putting his hands on her?" Indie snarled through the speaker.

"What?" Joey and Ricky shouted together.

"Say less," Joey muttered. "Fuck a probation my nigga."

"According to Senior he raped her...that motherfucka gotta die."

Thanks to Maria, Indie got Malcolm's location and Bookie, Rodney, Joey and Ricky were waiting in the parking lot for him to pull up. Indie parked his rental a block away and walked down to where the four of them were gathered. He dapped each of them with his free hand and held a gas can with the other before he blew past them and went to bang on Malcolm's door.

Indie didn't even bother covering his face, he wanted Malcolm to look at him like a man and not cower like a bitch until it was time for him to do so. Mid pound, Malcolm pulled the door open and looked Indie up and down. Indie noticed the rings around his eyes, chuckled and started dousing the gasoline into his house.

"The fuck are you doing?" Malcolm asked trying to push Indie back.

"Looks like someone already got to your ass but I'm about to rearrange all your shit." Indie's long arms started to extend letting his fist land wherever they did on Malcolm's face. Indie got the first minute of play before Ricky, Joey, and Rodney tagged themselves in.

"I heard you like to put your hands on women," Bookie rumbled propping himself on the wall and watching the four of them beat Malcolm senseless. "I can't stand a bitch nigga that likes to fight women and can't fight no niggas."

Bookie cracked his knuckles and licked his lips. "'Cause you run into niggas like me who don't give a fuck and like to...fuck with pretty bitches like you. In jail we call niggas like you...new booty. Sweet cheeks. Butter."

Indie stood up and wiped the sweat from his brow. "Bookie, he is all yours."

Joey, Ricky, and Rodney stood up and walked past Bookie who was unzipping his khakis. Malcolm was sprawled out across the floor groaning in pain. Before Indie could fully walk out the house, he spit on him. Walking out and closing the door behind him, he stood at the door with his back turned to it and his jaw clenched.

A loud grunt sounded through the door followed by a simultaneous scream of agony. Malcolm's screams were blood-curdling and they didn't stop until Bookie did. Minutes later, Bookie walked out and wiped the sweat from his face. "That nigga ain't talkin'."

"Bet," Indie responded, handing him a roll of cash. "Thanks for looking out."

Rodney and Bookie walked away leaving Indie, Joey, and Ricky standing there. Indie pulled out a blunt, lit it with a match, opened the door to Malcolm's small apartment. He flicked it inside. "Goodnight bitch. Let's go."

They walked back up the block and looked at each other. None of them were going to discuss this, this was just everything else. "Get back to L.A. Baby and I will be back tomorrow. Joey, there's some furniture being delivered to Radius180, oversee that for me."

CHAPTER SIXTEEN

Taj

A soft knock on the door caught Taj's attention. She stood on her counter top in the kitchen pulling the unused dishes down to pack. Packing the kitchen was easy. She didn't use anything in it, so everything was still in boxes except for her glasses, plates and bowls. All the things that Indie really needed at his place. She jumped off the counter and glanced at her iPad and reviewed the cameras to make sure it wasn't Malcolm. Although he hadn't been popping up, she wanted to err on the side of caution. It was better for everyone involved if he just stayed away. Her face lit up when she saw Indie on the other side with a duffle bag draped over his shoulder. Taj scurried to the door to open it and throw her arms around his shoulders.

Indie nuzzled his face into the crook of her neck while he bent over to wrap his arms around her petite frame. He placed a kiss to her bare shoulder and stepped forward into her condo. "Damn you smell good."

Taj released him, closed the door, and gently bit her lip with excitement. "I always smell good."

"You know thank you, babe, always works," he chuckled standing between the kitchen and the living room. "This is dope as fuck, though. I love the color."

"Of course, you do." Taj took his bag and walked into her bedroom with it. "It was something I did as a reminder. Even though I couldn't see you I needed to be reminded."

Those words made Indie's chest tight and his heart contract a little. He rubbed his chest and walked into the room behind her. "Every room?"

"Every room." Taj's reply was as soft as her eyes when they landed on him. "Like I said, I looked for you in places. Some places I hid you in. Like the color. No one knew why I wanted blue walls in every room but I knew."

Connecting with him, she laid her head on her chest. "Anyway, I don't want to make this heavy. Just..."

Indie pulled away slightly and tugged gently on her hair so her face would be titled toward him. "Nah, it's good. You're good. I understand."

A soft kiss to the lips was welcomed by Taj before she stepped away. "I'm going to order some food. You get comfortable."

As she was getting ready to walk out of the room, Indie caught her by her arm and motioned her back to him. He craned his neck down to look at her tenderly, pushing his hand through her hair and kissing her forehead.

Taj looked at him and knew that there was something he wasn't telling her. But she learned that he would tell her everything when he was ready so she didn't press the issue. Instead she wrapped her tiny hand around his and kissed his red knuckles. "Go get comfortable. I'm going to order food."

Pulling herself away from him she set out the room to order food, find a movie and finish packing up the kitchen. Indie emerged from the room almost thirty minutes later with a pensive expression on his face. Taj was taking the take out containers out of the bag and placing them on the counter. Hearing the door to the master bedroom open, she popped her head up.

"I got Thai. There's a spot up the block that I love," she started.

Opening a container of curry and rice she fixed their plates and sat at the counter top on a bar stool.

Indie mumbled, "Thanks."

The first ten minutes of dinner was quiet. Nothing but the sound of their forks hitting the plate. Indie dropped his fork and looked at Taj. "Why didn't you tell me he put his hands on you?"

Taj slowly lifted her head to face Indie. She released a sigh and twirled her fork around on her plate. "Because...I knew what would have happened if I did. And it didn't matter anymore it was over."

Indie shook his head no. "It's never that easy, Baby. There's a code that I live by. Protect your head, protect your woman, and protect your family no matter the costs. Off the strength of that alone, I could never let it slide."

"Babe," Taj spoke up dropping her fork and closing her eyes. "My life with Malcolm is one that I tried to move through. Feeling absolutely nothing. And for a while I managed... as long as I managed it was fine. But every year it got harder. But after you showed back up it turned into hell. I didn't tell anyone. What was it going to change? It was a push I needed to be able to close the door. The door is closed, the house is sold, and I'm sitting right here ready and willing to walk into forever with you. Please, let this be the last time we bring it up."

Indie stood up from the stool and stood behind her. "I won't have to bring it up because it's handled. All I want to do for the rest of the night is to hold you. Can you let me do that?"

"You never have to ask."

He brushed his lips against her skin and pulled himself away. "I wonder sometimes how a nigga like me got so lucky to have someone like you."

"Not lucky. You got blessed because I'm a gift. You better know it," she commented with a playful slap to the chest.

As the night went on Taj enjoyed having Indie in her arms and his head resting on her chest. They joked, shared their new dreams and enjoyed the love that wrapped them up in a blanket of warmth. She felt her pieces coming together, but her core was missing.

THEY WERE BACK in L.A. and Indigo insisted that they ride around and enjoy what was left of the summer before fall completely took over but the air was nippy. "Where are we going?"

"Baby," Indie softly groaned.

Kicking her feet up on the dash she hummed. "I know, I know...enjoy the ride."

Indie chuckled and looked over at her heeled feet kicked up on the dash. He knew that she was going to be a problem when she walked out the house in the pleated mini skirt and ankle boots. Now that her feet were on the dash and her thighs were exposed it wasn't going to be easy to keep his focus.

He pulled into the parking lot of Radius180 and parked his car. "Come in here with me real quick. We got an hour before our dinner reservation."

Taj drew her legs back in and placed them on the seat

before she placed them on the floor of the car. "You should love how I follow you blindly."

"Trust is a hell of a drug ain't it?" Indie chuckled climbing out the car and strolling around the car with his slight limp. Taj knew that it was something that annoyed him at times but she thought it was sexy. When he strolled around the car to her side, she watched him with a lustful twinkle in her eyes before he opened her door. "Why you lookin' at me like that?"

"Like what?" Taj questioned innocently as she took his hand and pulled herself up out of the car. "I just like the way you look…"

"I'm not playin' with you," he chuckled. "I'm hungry and I'm not getting caught up in you before we get to dinner. You know what you're doin'."

"I'm not doing nothing," Taj spoke up with a sly smirk across her face. She followed Indie to the front door of the building and stood to his side while he opened it. The way she positioned herself made him take note. She could see him and see anything coming up behind him.

His smirk was soft as she pulled the door open for her and let her walk in front of him. Taj sauntered into the building being sure to sway her hips just right so she could hold his attention. She was playing a game that was more than likely going to get her bent over a railing, but she didn't mind at all. That's what she wanted. She wanted to bring out the freaky side of Indie.

There wasn't a layer of him that she didn't adore. The cool side of Indie was what captivated her. She needed the stillness of his spirit when they first connected. The protectiveness he embodied along with the savage that could be brought out by simply throwing off the balance of his family. Most of all the way he loved her with all of his layers made him irresistible to her.

Taj stepped into the building and looked around at the tables, chairs and desks stacked up on the far side of the building. "Is this it?"

"It is," he answered with a smile. "Radius 180."

"Radius 180?" Taj repeated.

Indie licked his lips and locked the door before taking a couple of steps toward her. He took her hand and led her up the stairs so she could see the entire gander of the building. "My life came back full circle from almost being snatched away...Radius. Then I turned it around and I'm not going back to my old ways...180."

He molded his arms around her body and grinned into her hair. "I wanted you to see what you poured your money into."

Taj's eyes lit up with pride for him. Admiration for him. Happiness and joy, for him. "I'm so damn proud of you."

"I couldn't have done it without you," he muttered prompting her to turn around and look up at him

"Stop saying that." Her voice was soft but it was powerful enough to make him stop breathing. "You did this. You would have found a million ways to get this done without me. This is your vision and your legacy. You dreamed about this and you did it. I don't have enough words in my vocabulary to tell you how proud I am. Just to know that everything that tried to kill you only made you stronger. You say you're lucky to have me, but Indie... you're a gift. You're my gift. And to experience this with you right now is my blessing."

The look in Indigo's eyes was softer than cashmere. The tear that inched down her cheek was brushed away before he hovered his lips over hers. It was a slow passionate kiss. Taj's body was pressed against the railing and Indigo. Her hands were fused into the sides of his face and his hands gripped the root of her hair.

"Dinner is going to have to wait," he mumbled between the

smacking of their lips. Trailing his hand up her skirt, he gripped her ass before lifting her leg and prompting her to hook it around his leg. His fingers hooked the seat of her panties and pulled them to the side. Sliding two fingers in without warning, Indie chuckled at how wet she was and gliding them in and out slowly while she moaned and held on to him to support herself.

As sensational as his long fingers felt dipped inside of her river, she wanted him...all of him. Removing her hands from his shoulders to the zipper on his jeans. Tugging at his belt, then the button of his jeans and the zipper, Taj was finally able to free him.

Taj wrapped both of her legs around his waist and held on to him as he waddled over to the wall so he could have his way with her. She took his lips back into hers and felt himself position himself at her opening. She crashed her body down on his and released one of the loudest, seductive, euphoria laced moans that reverberated off the walls of the building. They were both on a mission, to make the other cum as fast as they could. She happily used her inner thigh muscles to squeeze her legs around him and bounce up and down on his dick.

The faster she went, the heavier he moaned which only made her wetter. "Got damn."

"You feel so good," Taj moaned her songs of praises.

Pressing his hand against the wall, Indie continued to stroke through Taj's waves of orgasms before he finally released one of his own. They panted and held onto each other until the feeling subsided. "Shit," Indie huffed using the strength he had left to place Taj on the desk and pull his pants up.

He disappeared from her sight into the bathroom to get hand towels and wet them with warm water. Taj laid lazily on the desk while Indie cleaned himself up and came back out to do the same to her. "I'm not fucking around with you again until I eat. I fucked all my energy out."

Taj giggled as he kissed the inside of her calf and then leaned up to kiss her. "It's these damn boots."

"I knew you would like them," she hummed sitting up and scooting to her feet. "Come on, let's go eat now that we've broken your building in."

Arriving at the restaurant just in time to make their reservation, they were seated in the far corner of the dining room.

"How you feelin' Baby?" Indie questioned looking over the table at her. She had zoned out for a minute and it wasn't until Indie started talking that she came back.

She shook her head and smiled faintly. "Nothing, I'm good."

He frowned.

"Baby..."

"What?"

"We're not doing that...I'm connected to you. I know when it's something," Indie vocalized making her eyes flutter.

"As angry as I am with him... I miss him," she admitted blinking her tears away. "He's still my dad...although he can be an asshole sometimes."

Indie leaned on his elbows and looked at her. "I think it's time for you to put your pride aside and talk to him. I get a feeling that there is a lot about him that you don't know."

Taj frowned and pushed her hands through her hair. "I don't want to go on like this. Everything that I can feel and see, I want it. Life is too short for me to be angry with him all the time."

Indie smiled because he didn't have to do much work to get her to fold. "It's time to talk to him and heal this. I want everything that's good for you. Your father, despite how I feel about the nigga, is good for you."

Taj's face flashed a grim expression. The tears sprung back in her eyes and threatened to spill over the brim. "I know."

SAMMIE: DON'T WAKE ME UP

Don't wake me up if I'm dreaming
Rather not know, just leave me so
Don't wake me up, now I ain't leaving
I'm staying with you babe
Don't wake me up

CHAPTER SEVENTEEN

*S*enior

His heart sat in his stomach and his palms were sweaty. He rubbed his hands over the fabric of his denim jeans and waited for Taj to walk through the door. When Indie called him the night before and told him to be at Mary's house, his heart immediately dropped. He hadn't laid his eyes on Taj since he left San Francisco before all hell broke loose. Senior hated that their relationship had boiled down to this. If he looked back on the journey that led them here, he could see the disconnect. Taj was already holding on to him by a thread before Bubba died. Now it severed and he could only pray that this initial conversation would lead to many more.

"Drink this and calm down," Mary muttered handing her brother a glass of whatever. "Have you got any idea what you're going to tell that girl?"

"No." His voice was no higher than a whisper.

Mary hummed and put her hands on her hip. "I suggest starting with the truth. She deserves to know who you really are."

"I've buried that part of me the night I left here."

"And you dug it up when you came back," Mary countered. "It's enough of the bullshit, Chucky. It's enough of this."

"Mary," Senior groaned taking a gulp of the water and sitting back on the couch. "I don't need to hear you fuss. You sound like mom."

"Good, maybe it's her telling you to tighten up," Mary made a groan of her own push up her throat and out her mouth.

Senior opened his mouth to reply back to her but the front door opened and Taj walked in behind Indie. He sprang to his feet and looked at his daughter who was casually dressed in a royal blue L.A. Dodgers t-shirt and gray joggers. The Nike sneakers on her feet and the ponytail on her hair led him to believe that she wasn't with the games today. That and the look on her face she studied him over like a science project.

"Taj," he spoke up breathlessly. He shifted nervously from side to side studying how she held Indie's hand as a sense of security.

Indie surveyed the room before turning around to face Taj. Senior could still see her apprehensive stature while Indie leaned down and started whispering something inaudible in Taj's ear. Whatever he was telling her loosened her scowl up just a bit and it relaxed her hiked shoulders. He followed it up with a kiss to her cheek and a soft brush of the cheek.

"You're good, Baby. Just remember what I told you," Indie mumbled before taking a step back and looking at Aunt Mary and Senior. "Y'all good?"

Mary nodded her head and Senior did the same. He caught Indie's eye, there was no need in repeating his thank you. Indie knew what it was and so did he.

Taj nodded her head and smiled faintly at him before she rested her eyes on her aunt. "Hey Auntie."

"Hey Baby," Mary beamed as she wrapped her arms

around her. "Indie and me are going to leave you two alone. Try not to tear up my house."

Taj chuckled softly and nodded her head. "I'll try my best."

Senior waited for the two of them to walk out the door before motioning for Taj to sit down next to him. Instead she sat in the chair that was furthest away from him, declining his silent invitation. "You can start wherever you like."

Senior ran his hand through his beard and grunted. "There's no other place to start than the truth I guess."

"You've guessed correctly," Taj mumbled. "You're smart...you just don't be thinking."

Senior chuckled. He used to tell Bubba that all the time. "You're right."

"Mm... come on, Senior, don't do this. I already feel a way about being here," she admitted looking into Senior's somber face. "One on hand, I miss you 'cause all that's left is me and you...but on the other hand it is very hard to see past what you did. I don't understand it and it's been very hard to continue to love you."

Senior dropped his eye contact with her, brushed his hands over her face and sighed. "I've done so many things in my life that I regret. You can't even begin to..."

"Tell me." Taj bluntly cut him off. "Outside of you being a pain in my ass I don't know who you really are..."

"Baby," Senior huffed trying to rid himself of the pain in his chest. He sat back in the cushions and tried focusing on everything else but her. "The day we pulled up to this house and you walked up the steps, and Indigo laid his eyes on you...I knew I was up for a fight. And the fight wasn't really with him or with you. But that's how I made it. I didn't see that maybe this guy dressed in blue dickies, and that flag hanging out his pocket could have a dream and was just trying to make it out alive the only way he knew how. All I saw was me."

Taj's ear perked. Now Senior had her attention. "Huh? Stop playing Daddy. I don't have time for this."

She started to stand up but Senior's voice made her freeze.

"Sit down Taj Ali. I am still your daddy. No matter how angry you are with me. I am still your daddy and you're going to sit your stubborn ass right there and listen to what I have to say."

Taj's eyes squinted and she pressed her lips together.

"I've seen death, Baby. Unfortunately, so have you. I never intended for you to have to experience it so many times. When I married your mother, I promised her the world. When Bubba was born, I did the same. But you. You were special and you gave your mother hell from the second we conceived you until the second she gave birth to you. I remember holding you close and promising that I would never leave you, that I will love you and show you the right way, and protect you. I feel... I know I've failed you. Hell, all four for you..."

"Four?" Taj questioned confused.

Senior nodded his head and hummed to himself. "We'll get to that. Let me finish. You have been right. I let Bubba sell drugs knowing that it could end his life at any moment. I never mourned your mother's death. But I watched you push through every loss and turn it into a win. I've watched you try and hold on to whatever piece of them that you could just so you could get through from day to day. I've watched you love so fiercely it made me feel like you didn't need me. You got something burning on the inside of you that just propels you forward."

Taj dropped her head and shook it. "You're wrong. I needed you. I needed you every day. And I get it. You lost mom and you changed. It was like your light died and you just went from day to day because you had me and Bubba. You checked out on us and you never checked back in. And then you get here and lost your damn mind."

He pinched the bridge of his nose and groaned. The silence was loud and he was trying to calm his thoughts before he told his daughter the real reason he didn't want her with the man she loved so much.

"Baby, I was Indie before. A young gang banger running around here wild. There was a night that my cousin and I went to serve some guys that came over here on some bullshit. My cousin didn't make it... I did. And I ran. I never wanted to look back. Thinking about you with Indie scared the shit out of me and that night when they shot up that car with you in it was the scariest moment of my life," Senior voice began to shake. "Because if I were to lose you then there would be no reason for me to live anymore. So yeah, I panicked. I needed to get you away from here and him and distract you. I fucked up. I knew you were pulling away from Malcolm but I figured if I bribed him, he would give you a reason to stay and I was wrong."

"Dead ass wrong," Taj muttered. "Had you told me, I would have chosen for myself and I wouldn't have been this angry. That shit really hurt me. You were supposed to be the one to put me back together again but I did it myself. When I learned that I could...I didn't need anyone to say that they loved me and treat me like shit. I did enough of that to myself. While I was looking for Indie... I was looking for you. Because I was sure you saw me hurting and you would just wrap your arms around me and tell me that I was going to get through it. I feel like I lost everything and all I had was me."

"I carry all of that pain everyday Taj. The pain of letting him down, your mother, your brother...you. I can't fix what I did with them but I can fix this. Tell me where to start," Senior pleaded.

"Just be my dad. That's it. At this point, I don't need you to raise me anymore. That's done and over. I need you to just be dad, show up when I need you to show up. Hug me and tell me that I can make it through whatever. Tell me you're proud of me. And accept that I am going to be with Indigo regardless. You two both have room and competing with him or trying to keep me from him isn't going to work anymore."

Senior nodded his head. "I see. I've read him all wrong. He's a better Crip than I am."

"No," Taj mumbled. "Indie is a man. A better man than he was before. The thing is, that when he had to come back and face the shit he did, he didn't let up. When he had the option of reverting, he fought against it. There is a difference between being a gang banger and a gang member. Let go of the shit you didn't do and start doing shit that matters. Eventually, I can forgive you for the things you've done. It won't be immediate but I'll get there."

"You know I love you."

"I know and I know that love can make you crazy and irrational. I love you but I don't like you," Taj commented. "You should hug me now..."

Senior grunted as he pushed himself up to embrace his daughter. He took one step toward her and she stood up and wrapped her arms around his waist. Senior tried to hold himself together but his emotions quickly took over him. His head rest on top of hers and he squeezed his eyes shut. "Baby girl, I love you and I am so sorry I failed you."

Taj's face was pressed into his chest and she released tears of her own. "One last shot. You better make it count okay?"

Senior kissed the top of her head and muttered, "Okay."

CHAPTER EIGHTEEN

*I*ndie

After walking up and down the block with Mary, Indie sat on the steps of the porch and waited for Taj to walk out. Or for an ambulance to come scoop Senior's beaten body off the floor. He scrolled through his phone to distract himself until then. Indie was serious about giving her all the time she needed to talk to her father.

He tried to get his thoughts from getting the best of him. If he had the same opportunity that Taj had, would he take it? If he saw his father again what would he do? What would he say? Indie made a way for himself without him. He made a way for Joey without him so what point would he serve now? Especially after Indie was raised by the streets because he couldn't be a man and be there for the family that he created.

The metal door opened and Taj mumbled something over her shoulder that made Indie turn around and stand to his feet.

"I'm going back on Sunday, you should make yourself available before then," Taj's voice fully pulled Indie out of his thoughts.

"I got it," Senior rumbled entering his sight. "Indie."

"Senior," Indie replied with a nod of the head. He almost called him Chucky but he didn't know what he told or didn't tell Taj so he kept it to himself. "You ready baby?"

"Yeah." Taj smiled up at Indie softly. "I'll see you later."

"Y'all be safe," Senior ordered while Taj walked down the steps of the house to the car.

She climbed in and pulled her phone from the cup holder and started looking through emails. Indie climbed behind the steering wheel and started the engine. Taking her phone from her hands and dropping it back in the cup holder he examined the dried tears on her face. "Talk to me, Baby. You good?"

"Yeah," she replied softly. "I'm good. I'm hungry."

"Tacos?"

"Tacos are always the move." She buckled her seatbelt and closed her eyes. Indie could feel the emotion course through her so he let her enjoy the silence that surrounded them until later.

He knew just what to do to get her out of her feelings or at least let her talk through them. Traveling down the street, Indie spotted the taco truck and whipped the car into the parking lot.

"You remember when I brought you here the first time?" He chuckled remembering their first date that ended with a bang. He watched Taj's face perk up. "You inhaled those tacos like you never ate good food before."

"Well... I can't cook and Senior was working so technically I hadn't." Smacking her lips, she unbuckled her seatbelt and rolled her eyes. "And plus, I never had Cali tacos. They hit different. I'm surprised I haven't turned into a taco."

"I mean that wouldn't be a bad thing," he muttered to himself as he climbed out of the car. He walked around the car and opened her door.

"What did you mumble?" Taj popped her eyebrow and climbed out the car. "Speak up, say that with your chest, nigga."

Indie threw his head back in laughter before closing her door and hanging his arm over her shoulder. He leaned into her and pressed his lips against her ear and repeated himself. "I said, I mean it isn't a bad thing... because I'd eat you all the time."

Taj giggled lightly and bit her lip before looking up at him with a twinkle in her eyes. "You already do that. So, let me just morph into a taco."

"Where did my good girl go?"

"You turned her out." Taj shrugged her shoulders. "And I'm a grown ass woman."

"And I'm a grown ass man. But you'll always be my girl. You'll always be that wide eyed, shy girl with the beats wrapped around her neck that I met on the porch of Mary's house. The girl who tried to ignore me like a nigga didn't exist. But I got that didn't I? Tagged and bagged it. Graffitied my name on that."

"You did something," Taj sassed. "You really did something. You got me to tattoo your name on me...so you're right. It's your turn."

"My turn for what?" he questioned with a puzzled expression.

"Tatt my name so I know it's real."

"Now I know you really trippin'." He chuckled before ordering their tacos.

Taj drew her neck back and pinned her brows together. "Why are you actin' like Diane didn't give you good sense? I'm not tripping on nothing. You can either tattoo my name or I can cover this up. Pick your poison, babe. But know if I cover this up, you'll be best friends with your hand and some lotion."

Indie scoffed and hissed. "Shhhhiiiitttttt...I've gone to jail. My hand and lotion ain't ever let me down."

Taj burst out laughing and walked away from him. "I can't stand you."

"You got to be ready, Baby," he chuckled paying for their food. "That ain't a problem. We'll head over to Loco after we finish up here."

"Wait." Taj halted her laughter. "I was playin'."

"No, you weren't. You meant it and it's cool. I'll put your name wherever you want it, Baby. Ain't no shame in my game. None at all." Indie placed a quick kiss to her lips and pulled away so he could see her smile from ear to ear. "That's that shit I like."

After they ate, Indie drove them over to Loco's tattoo shop to get some more work done. They walked into the building hand in hand and Loco walked out from the back with a blunt between his lips. "Azul?"

"What up nigga!" Indie greeted throwing his hand up. A warm smile stretched across his face from ear to ear that radiated throughout the room. That was a part of his power. Whatever room he walked into illuminated with his aura.

Taj released his hand and let him greet Loco so she could go look through his art books.

Loco came around the counter and pulled her into a brotherly hug. "I heard you were back and you didn't even come and see me. I should put your ass out my shop."

They separated and Indie leaned on the counter. "You know how this shit goes. I needed to lay low then I needed to make moves but I'm here."

"I see you got your lady." Loco beamed with happiness to see his old friend.

Indie smirked over his shoulder watching Taj get lost in the artwork. "She's the real deal man. Ain't never had nothing like that in my life."

"Don't let it go either. It's not every day you meet a woman that don't make you question her motives. You know we grew up real skeptical. She makes you comfortable?"

"Hell yeah."

"She held you down?"

"For sure."

"She solid? Ten toes down and accepts you for everything you are and everything you're not?"

"On hood."

"Lock that down immediately. Niggas out here kill for women like that. I know I'll kill about mine."

Indie nodded his head with a smirk and stood straight up. "That ain't even an issue. I'll be working on that. But for today, I got to get a piece done for her."

Loco nodded his head in agreement. "What you thinking about?"

"You know they shot me and missed my heart? That's the only spot that isn't fully tatted yet. Let's do a blue heart around the scar with her name." Indie looked back over his shoulder and admired Taj before drawing her attention to him. "Hey, Baby. What you getting?"

"A blue heart works for me," she replied without looking up at him.

"Do you need a shot?" Loco asked.

"Nah, I'm cool," Taj hummed.

Heading back to the booth, Taj sat down first and put her hand on the table. "Left hand fourth finger."

Indie rose his brow. Taj smirked and said, "Marriage is cool, but I've learned to live for right now because I don't know if I'll have you tomorrow. But for today, I'll show you that it's forever. However long or short that may be."

That comment made his chest tight. A feeling he hadn't felt in a couple months. "Damn girl. You riding for real?"

"Until the wheels fall off."

Almost three hours later they were back at Mary's house waiting on Ricky and Ajai to come over for dinner. Indie sat on the porch between Taj's thighs and looked at the heart she got tatted on her finger. He'd been complimenting how good it looked from the time she got it til now.

"Where is this nigga? They always late." Indie grumbled breaking down the bud on his lap with the gutted Backwoods.

"Let me do that," Taj offered holding her hand out.

"Baby you don't know what the hell you're doing."

"I do. Give it here." Indie scrunched up his face and handed it over. "Don't look at me like that."

"Who taught you that?" he questioned in confusion and shock as she broke it down and started to roll it.

Taj snickered and rolled her tongue over the back slowly locking eyes with him. "I be watching you."

"Baby," he warned unable to take his eyes off of her. "You better quit it."

She released another snicker and focused back on rolling his blunt perfectly.

"It's almost been five years, Baby. When you came strutting your fine ass up these steps," he started up again looking around the hood at the kids playing.

"What did you think about when you looked into my eyes?" Taj asked between rolling.

Indie nervously chuckled. "I'm not telling you."

"I will mess up this roll so bad," she threatened.

Indie scoffed. "Stop playin' girl."

"Tell me... please." She almost whined but it was low and seductive and turned Indie into putty.

"I saw my life in your eyes. I saw purpose. I saw forever.

This place would have killed us if we let it. But we didn't. That night when I shielded you and I felt how tight you held on to me, I knew that that wasn't the end. It couldn't be. I felt myself fading in and out and I just had to hold on because I couldn't leave you. I knew from the day you stood here that I couldn't leave you. You are special..."

"Who knew that you were so damn emotional." Taj snickered kissing the top of his head.

"Thug love is the best love, baby. I'll remind you again tonight when we get home and I bend you over."

Taj smirked and handed Indie his blunt. "You're welcome."

"You got to hit this since you rolled it," he commented after lighting it. "Here."

"Uhh." Taj paused.

"Nah, don't bitch up now. Take a hit."

Taj took the blunt back from his fingers and inhaled a puff and started coughing. "Oh my God."

"Don't swallow it baby." Indie groaned before laughing at her hit her chest. "Watch."

Taking it from her fingers he puffed, held it in his cheeks and blew it into the air. Taj tried again; this time much smoother than the first. "There you go."

CHAPTER NINETEEN

*T*aj

    She couldn't get Indie in the house quick enough before her hands were taking possession over his body. They claimed their territory followed by her lips trailing them. Taj was stumbling backward trying to get his belt loose so she could free him and have her way. Taj moaned hungrily as though she'd been deprived of the dick. It was something about the electricity she felt when they connected that she couldn't get enough of. It surged through her body causing her to be commanded by no one but him.

However, Indie had different plans for her. Fucking her was always fun but tonight the atmosphere around them was different. It could have been because they both had OG Kush and Crown in their systems. Taj wanted him now and Indie wanted to take his time with her. She would have to allow him to meet her halfway to create a beautiful mid-tempo beat for both of them to vibe to.

Indie firmly grabbed her hands and shook his head. "Stop."

"What's wrong?" she asked breathlessly. Her face flooded with uncertainty as she watched Indie look back at her with low eyes. His glare was hypnotizing her. As bad as she wanted to reach out and finish everything she started, she couldn't. Indie's hold on her was changing the course of control.

"Nothing," he mumbled. "It's not about me tonight. It's all about you. I want to take care of you. You've selflessly given me everything. I'm going to let you go and I want you to walk upstairs and get naked. Lay in the middle of the bed on your stomach and wait on me."

Taj tucked her bottom lip into her teeth right before Indie took possession of her lips and released her. As much as she didn't want to listen, she complied. The rewards of her listening to him for the moment would be greater in the end.

She pushed herself up the stairs and quickly stripped down and rushed into the shower. A quick shower and oil down, she made her way to the bed in anticipation of feeling him. Minutes went by and the longer she rested in the pillows, the heavier her eyes grew. Taj drifted in and out of sleep. Eventually, sleep won.

The time that passed between her falling asleep and Indie's hands roaming over her body was unknown. She squirmed in her sleep feeling Indie's soft kisses trail from the base on her neck, down her bare back, and over her ass cheeks. A flicker of his thick tongue over the crevice made her release a deep moan that woke her up. Taj tried to shake the sleep from her eyes while Indie pushed her legs open and devoured her from the back.

Neither drunkenness or the high from the weed had worn off and the pleasure he was inducing was mind numbing. Taj buried her head in the pillows and moaned in pleasure. Indie pushed his face into her honey pot further and hummed in delight.

Taj felt his hands grace her flesh while he consumed her. The orgasm was approaching and both of them braced for the impact of it. When it hit, it was intense. Taj lifted her face from the pillow and the sound she was trying to hold back came flowing back out in a roar. He continued to run his tongue over her center until the quake subsided.

"Tell me what you want." Indie's seductive tone filled the dark room. "I want you to say it."

"Give me everything," Taj slurred feeling the length of Indie's fingers run along her opening. "All of you. All of it. Right now."

Indie smirked into the darkness and positioned himself to dive deep inside of her causing her to roar again in ecstasy. His body glided over hers with ease. Taj was boxed in between Indie's elbows and she bit the pillow. His breath on her neck made the euphoria heighten. Her flower leaked nectar for him.

Indie's husky voice in her ear while he hit her spot over again made her body pulsate around him. "Yeah, Baby. Just like that."

"I'm going to cum baby," Taj cried into the pillow. Her body was shaking and the emotion that was built in her chest was coming out in a flood. Taj's tears soaked the pillow. She held on to the pillow as tight as she could.

Indie's pace remained steady. He placed sensual kisses to her earlobe, the curve of her neck, and her shoulder. "Keep it right there."

Indie released a chime of moans into her ear and locked his fingers with hers.

"Stop teasing me," Taj whispered through her tears and the buildup of her orgasm.

Indie chuckled followed by a moan and continued through with his calm, collected, and cool strokes. Taj hiked her leg up more letting him have full access to her spot. She gripped the pillow and let the wave of spine-tingling pleasure rush over her.

He rumbled. "I feel that. Give it all to me. We not done yet."

The rest of the night went on into the early realms of the morning and Taj rested tiredly on his side with her head tucked in the cradle of his arm. She kissed his rib cage and ran her fingers along his tattooed midsection.

Indie's eyes remained closed when he asked, "Talk to me. You should be knocked out after all of that. What's going on?"

"I am starving." Taj chuckled sitting up and hovering her body over him to grab her phone. "That's what I'm thinking about."

Indie laughed lightly and watched her peck away on her phone. "The munchies are kicking in now, aren't they?"

"Hell yeah," she muttered exploring her options in the Postmates app. "Burgers, tacos, breakfast...chicken...breakfast with chicken and a milkshake."

Indie frowned his face up. "Baby, what?"

"What? You want some too? I'll order two of everything."

Indie laughed again and sat up on the edge of the bed. Taj watched him out of the corner of her eye as she looked at his phone and let out a sigh. His shoulders slumped a bit before he caught himself and straightened up. She watched as he palmed his face, scratched his beard and peeked over his shoulder.

"That'll be cool," he responded as he grabbed a blunt from the box and stood up. Indie pulled a pair of shorts on and shuffled out of the room.

Her eyes trailed him until he disappeared. Whatever was happening with him she was going to pull it out. It wasn't work related because he left his phone behind and his skin didn't glow red. Instead his peaceful energy had turned sad.

Taj pushed herself out of the bed, grabbed a shirt and found him sitting outside on the balcony blowing smoke into the air with his feet kicked up on the railing. Stepping out into the dawn, she placed her hands on his shoulders and massaged them lightly. The tightness of them alarmed her. From his shoulders, she traveled her soft hands over his skin to his neck and continued to massage until a heavy sigh escaped through his lips.

"Where did you go?" she softly droned in his ear. "Say something."

Indie tried to hold it in and not let her into his head, but it was always a game he played and lost. Taj had the keys to his heart, soul, mind and body. And when she requested to enter them, he let her roam freely.

"It's my pops birthday...same day he walked out."

Taj's hands stayed on his neck as she walked around to look into his eyes. She lowered herself in front of him and lightly touched the side of his face. "While we're healing things with the people we love, it might be time for you to reach out to him. And before you tell me no, just listen and hear me out okay? Reach out and ask to meet at a neutral location. Say your piece and see if he has anything he wants to say. If not, you did your part and you can let it go."

Indie dragged his eyes from the ocean to Taj. His eyes grew soft the second they locked. "You're right. He doesn't owe me nothing more than an explanation."

"Then don't leave until he gives you everything he owes."

Indie licked his dry lips and looked down at her gazing up at him. "Why do you know what to say?"

Taj stood up and lowered herself into the chair next to him. "I just know that there are things that you need closure on and who would I be not to give you back everything you've given me? The beauty of being in a relationship with someone who wants the best for you and the best of you. They won't accept anything less than that."

"And what about the ugly parts?"

"Your ugly parts are only fueled by the passion of the good parts that haven't been communicated properly." Taj finalized her statement with a shoulder shrug.

CHAPTER TWENTY

*I*ndie
For a brief second Indie regretted listening to Taj's bright-eyed idea to meet with his father. Although he knew it was needed, he sat in the parking lot of the mom and pop restaurant talking himself out of going inside. The lull of the engine and the racing of his thoughts kept him from climbing out. Unknowingly, he rolled his lips against one another and stared into space.

"We gettin' out of this car or what?" Joey questioned breaking Indie's focus. "You good?"

For the sake of saving face and showing Joey that he wasn't fazed at all about this meeting, he swallowed his fear and opened the door to the car. "Yeah, I'm cool. Let's go in here so we can get this shit over with."

Killing the engine, Indie swung his long legs and climbed out. He scanned the area with a tight jaw while Joey did the same. Once he saw their father sitting at the table outside the small eatery, Indie released a heavy sigh. Their father stuck out like a sore thumb. All of the black and brown faces and their father was the only white one.

"Should we put this nigga out his misery and go over there and save his ass from getting jumped?" Joey questioned.

Indie leaned his elbows on the top of the car and shook his head. "Nah, let's see how much heart that nigga got."

"He doesn't have much," Joey muttered looking at their father with squinted eyes. "Let's get this over with. I'm not trying to be out here long talking to this nigga."

A grimace crossed Indie's face just as he stepped away from the car and shut the door. While he walked behind Joey, he hit the locks to his car and rubbed his chest. He hadn't looked his father in the eyes in years. It had been so long that he lost count. But Indie never forgot that day. It was one of the few things in his life that kept him up at night. And lately with Taj being around and working on repairing her relationship with her father, he thought about his more. However, he wasn't seeking a relationship from him. He was seeking closure. He needed it. But the closure just wasn't for him. It was for Joey too.

Joey needed to come to terms with who their father was and what he would never be. Indie figured that if Joey saw it with his own eyes, he would let his hate fall to the side and move forward with his life. Indie saw a spark in Joey. One that he thought Joey had lost years ago. But with Joey having another opportunity to turn his life around for good, Indie didn't want him taking anything from the past with them.

Upon reaching the table, they glanced at each other. Both of them looking calm, cool, and collected on the outside but a ball of unsettled, unsorted emotion on the inside. Their father stood to his feet and looked over his boys. His height, build, and posture was the same as Indie and Joey. The tightness in his jaw and intense glare he had made Indie feel like he was looking into a mirror.

And the tinge of redness in his skin let Indie know that he was just as nervous to meet up with them after so long. "Wow...it's like looking at myself."

Indie scoffed softly and Joey chuckled as they both took a seat ignoring his outstretched hand.

"Put that away. We don't shake hands of nigga's we don't respect," Joey replied. "You got something you need to say to us?"

"Well, I'm white so I'm not sure that would make me a n--"

"Watch your mouth, cuh," Joey spoke up again. "You around a bunch of hood niggas that want to jack you for nothin'. Don't let your vernacular get you fucked up out here in these streets."

Brenton narrowed his eyes before looking over his shoulder then back at Joey and Indie. "It's changed out here."

"Nah," Indigo spoke up. "It's the same. You just so happened to be fucking with a girl that had weight. Then you uprooted her from her life, married her and walked out on her and your sons. So, let's stop pretending like we are here to break bread and hold hands. We're not. It's been hell getting you to come and see us since you left. The only reason we're here today is to close the door."

Brenton inhaled deeply and looked at his sons with a hint of remorse. "I'm sorry about that. I couldn't imagine what it was like growing up ... here..."

"You mean in the hood? The neighborhood?" Joey questioned.

Indie could feel the anger radiating off of Joey. Instead of shutting him and the feelings he was entitled to down he let him have his moment. It was important that whatever Joey had on his chest be laid out on the table.

"What you're trying to say is that you're sorry you were a fuckin' piece of shit and a got damn coward. You left us and let this neighborhood raise us. You forced my momma to work three times harder just so she could barely get by. You turned your back on us," Joey fired off. "My brother was more of a father to me than you have ever been. This nigga gave up his life for me and you want me to sit here and talk to you like you're a man. You're nothin' but a white boy who came to the hood and found a pretty black girl to spend your time with."

"It wasn't like that, Joseph."

"Oh, it wasn't? So, what was it like when you walked out and didn't fuckin' look back? Huh? There's not a bone in you that's fuckin' sorry. I bet you got you a comfortable ass life while we were out here strugglin'. Lookin' to the OG's on the block to put us up on game cause the love we needed was chillin' livin' a better life than what we had."

Brenton shot Joey a glare that set him off. Springing to his feet, Joey flared his nostrils and stared down at him. "Fuck you lookin' at crazy?"

Indie stood to his feet and pushed Joey back. Looking at him in the eyes, Indie shook his head. "We not doin' this. Look at me. He already thinks that we aren't on his level. That's cool. Tell me what you want him to say to make it cool for you to walk away and not look back."

As hard as Joey was trying to be, Indie saw the little boy in him just wanting his father to accept him. Indie watched as his eyes filled to the brim with tears and his breathing increased. It broke Indie's heart. Up until now Joey had never shown how much their father not being there hurt him. Not like this.

Everyone around them disappeared. Indie's main concern was bringing Joey back down. He grabbed him by the back of his neck and pressed his forehead against his. "You good, bro. Just breathe. That nigga don't owe you shit but an explanation.

That's it. He don't have no power over you. Tighten up and poke your chest out."

Joey clenched his jaw and nodded his head before inhaling and pulling himself together. He tried but his thoughts escaped his lips making Indie's heart sink in the process. "Why didn't he want us? Why did he leave us here to get ate up like this? What did we do to him?"

Indie knew that it was only a matter of seconds until Joey became fully unhinged. He made the decision that he would walk Joey back to the car to calm his nerves. Indie would go get the answers that both of them sought.

"Just cool out, aight? I'll be back in a second."

Joey nodded slowly letting Indie know it was okay for him to walk away.

Indie returned to the table and looked at Brenton. "Look at me. In the face like a man."

Brenton cleared his throat and looked at Indie.

"It hurts me when my brother hurts. It hurt me when my mother cried herself to sleep behind you. It hurt when she had to choose between feeding us and making sure the lights stayed on. I dropped out of school so I could provide for my family. Something you didn't do. I don't know if you didn't try hard enough or you truly didn't give a fuck but it's cool. Everything you didn't do for him, I did. I wanted to have this sit down so I could look you in the face and tell you that without you, we made it. Self-made who took the stairs to get here. When you go to sleep at night with your new family, remember the one you left hanging who made it without you. I don't want your explanation; I don't need it. I'm cool. I don't wish no ill will on you 'cause without you I wouldn't be here. Your job is done. You're free and clear, aight?"

"I'm truly sorry you all had to grow up without me,"

Brenton delivered his half-baked apology that made Indie laugh.

"Nah. I'm sorry you didn't get you grow up with us. You missed out. We didn't."

He pulled himself away from the table and walked off to the car. "Get in, Joey. We're done."

The drive home was silent. Indie sped through the streets so he could get to the house and have a few moments to himself outside of Joey's presence. He didn't want to upset him anymore than he already was. Arriving home, Indie parked the car in the garage and made his way inside only to be met at the door by Taj.

His jaw tightened and his eyes fluttered. With a clenched jaw, Indie said, "I'm good."

Indie knew that Taj wasn't going to leave him alone as he took off to his unfinished office to have his space. She was right on his heels. Closing the office door behind them, she took a step toward him and put her hand on the center of his back. "Breathe."

Indie shook his head and groaned. "I'm good."

"Breathe," Taj repeated in the steadiest calming voice he'd ever heard from her. "Let it out. You can't hold on to that forever."

Indie sucked in air through his flared nostrils and tried to battle the tears and the burning sensation in his throat.

"Let it go," Taj couched. "Talk to me."

"I'm good."

"You're not good. I can feel your pain Indie and you got to let it go. Talk to me."

"He didn't want us...he didn't have to say it. That shit was all in his demeanor. He was ashamed that he even had us. You know how many nights I stood on a corner hustlin' with my stomach rumbling just so I could have some cash to make sure mom and Joey ate? I would lie and tell her I ate and I'm cool. You know how bad it hurt to get the game from OG's when my pops should've been the one giving it to me? That shit fucks you up. Who can do that to their kid?" he questioned letting the tears fall.

Taj took a step closer and wrapped her arms around his waist and kissed the middle of his back. Her touch kept him calm enough to sift through everything happening inside. "What hurt even more is seeing how bad it fucked Joey up. But I can't make no more scenario's up for him. He showed me who he was back then and I'm going to believe him now."

He dropped his head and put his hand over Taj's. "Thank you for trying."

"As long as you can move forward with that door closed, my job is complete. I would do it again."

"I know you would. That's why you can get whatever you want from me," Indie replied turning around to face her.

Taj reached up and wiped the tears from her face and hiked herself up to kiss his lips. "I'll let you chill for now. Your mom is coming over in a few hours to have dinner."

DINNER HAD COME and gone and the four of them found themselves on the back porch listening to the waves crash, eating cake and drinking.

"I heard about the meeting with your father. How'd that go?" Diane asked between bites of her cake. "Did he answer your questions?"

"He didn't need to answer them directly. We got the picture," Joey commented. "The nigga never wanted us. He walked out and let you raise us on your own. What kind of man does that to his kids? That's not a man I want to be."

Diane shrugged and looked at Indie and Joey. "You do understand that I have never had a problem with being all you two needed as far as parenting went? Yeah, things were rocky, but we made it because we stuck together. That's the beauty of all of this. You two learned to stick together even when you didn't want to. I know it sucks to finally realize that's the man he's become. But what's more important is the men that you have become. I will never take back any part of our journey together. That's what made us who we were and who we are. We are resilient. No matter what life has tried to throw at us, we made it. Remember that, don't forget it. From gang life to owning businesses to getting people off the streets. Honestly, fuck that nigga. He had everything in his life handed to him. You two had to take it the hard way and look how much you appreciate it."

Joey wrapped his arm around Diane's shoulders and kissed her cheek. "Thank you, Ma."

"Thank you, you two were my reason. And you've made me extremely proud to be your mother."

Indie and Joey had broken off to go smoke at the other end of the patio away from Diane, leaving Taj and Diane on the padded wicker patio sectional watching the waves crash and descend back and repeat. Indie watched his mother and the love of his life cuddle underneath the blanket and talk to each other.

"I am so happy you two worked this out. He has changed so much for the better," Diane spoke over her wine glass. "So, have you...you're calmer."

Taj smirked and dropped her head back. "I was angry for a very long time. It feels very good not to be carrying that anymore."

"How are you and Senior? I know your father is a pill, I've

experienced it first-hand, but he loves you. That I know. And love can make you do some crazy things."

"Love had me holding on to Indie for years."

"See." Diane pointed her finger at Taj. "So, you get it."

Taj lifted her head and nodded it. "I do. His number isn't blocked anymore. I pick up when he calls... so I'll get to the point to where I can forgive him. But I can't forget everything."

Diane wrapped her arm around Taj like she was her daughter. "And you shouldn't but know that he loves you. I love you and when you're here you're home."

Taj cuddled closer to her and responded, "I know."

SAMMIE: I WANT YOU

Baby girl, I love you and I felt the need to say it
There's sometimes we fuss and fight and baby girl, I hate it
You're my better half and you're sure appreciated
Never thought I'd settle down, without you, girl I'm naked
You're the only one that makes me feel like I do

CHAPTER TWENTY-ONE

*S*enior
   "And he opens doors," Maggie hummed taking Senior's hand and pulling herself out of the car. "Thank you."

"You're welcome." Senior smiled down at her softly and trailed her into Mary's house.

It was Thanksgiving Day, and everyone was huddled up in the kitchen ready to eat. The feeling in the house was warm and welcoming. Even Taj made an effort to hug his waist but when she looked over at Maggie her eyes squinted a bit.

"You brought a... friend," she commented giving Maggie a look over.

Senior knew that Taj hadn't given much thought to him moving on and this would probably be a shock to her. He prayed that she wouldn't be cold to Maggie. Especially now since they'd been spending more time together and things were starting to look and feel serious.

"Maggie," Senior started. "This is my very resilient daughter. Taj this is Maggie. We've been seeing each other for a while."

"Oh?" Taj asked with a grin taking over her lips. "Seeing each other or seeing each other."

"Taj Ali," Senior rumbled warningly.

"Daddy we are all grown here. If you are seeing her, I am very happy. That means you can stay out of my business. I just wish you introduced me to her a lot sooner than now. She's beautiful. Who knew you still had it in you?" Taj teased him.

Senior chuckled and kissed the top of her head. "You know I've always had it."

"Mm," Taj replied pulling away and extending her hand out to Maggie. "Maybe you and I should talk about him over a glass of wine. I can tell you all the secrets."

"Taj," he warned again but Taj was already in mid stride to pull Maggie away.

"She's fine Chucky," Mary spoke up. "You need to come and look at this turkey you stuck me with. And if it's done let's get ready to eat."

"Thank God!" Ricky grunted shooting up from his seat. "I've been waiting all day to eat."

Senior looked over at him and shook his head. "I thought I taught you how to check the turkey last year."

"Uncle Chuck...wasn't nobody paying attention to your disgruntled turkey teaching class last year," Ricky retorted making Indie snicker as he stood to his feet.

"How you doing?" Indie asked greeting him with a handshake and a half hug. Ricky's eyes widened looking at their embrace.

Over the last two months the more Taj allowed Senior back into her life, the more time he spent with both her and Indie. He was grateful for the opportunity to see the other side of Indie. The side that captured Taj's heart and refused to let it go.

"I'm good. How you? Businesses moving well?"

Indie nodded his head. "I need help with one though. When you got a second let me holla at you outside."

Senior saw Indie's eyes shift over to Taj who was in the small kitchen laughing with Maggie. He picked up on where Indie was headed and tried not to smile so big and jump to conclusions. "Aight, I got you."

"When did you two get so chummy?" Ricky questioned.

"Nigga chummy?" Indie questioned with a twisted face. "Who the fuck says that shit?"

"Listen..." Ricky started waving Indie off. "Let me live my life."

Joey walked up and laughed. "He smoked hella blunts earlier. I'm not fuckin' around with him."

"Me neither," Indie replied.

The afternoon went on with laughter and jokes over the table. Taj was still consumed with asking Maggie twenty-one questions. It made Senior's heart smile. She was taking a liking to Maggie. It happened almost instantly after Maggie explained to her that she would never try to take her mother's place and that she was happy just to have this moment and talk to her.

Senior knew had this been years ago Taj would have been a brat about the entire ordeal. But with time came changes and the maturity that Taj was exhibiting showed him that she was healing up the old wounds and moving forward.

While the women talked over wine and cake, Ricky and Joey played the PlayStation and Senior and Indie stood on the porch in the chilly autumn air.

"How's your new garage?" Indie asked. In the last few months Senior expressed to Indie that he was tired of working for other people and he wanted something of his own. Without a blink of an eye Indie went ahead and secured a place for Senior to call his own. The only stipulation was that Senior had to higher ex-gang members who were looking for another chance to do the right thing.

"Everything is going great. Those guys you sent over are really doing a great job," Senior shared.

"Imagine that." Indie chuckled. "Niggas went from boosting and jacking to doing legit business that feeds their families. All they need is a chance and a guide in the right direction."

"I really owe you for looking out."

"You don't owe me nothing. Don't mention it. It's the least we could do. We're responsible for all of these niggas out here. Not everyone is going to follow the way but if we can save one then we won. You know?"

Senior nodded his head. "I know, you're doing great things Indie."

"Appreciate it."

"How's that business treating you?" Senior asked.

Indie smiled from ear to ear as he dug in his pocket and handed Senior a ring box. "I wanted to come to you as a man and ask you. I'm not in the business of being a bitch and working around you. I know that your presence in her life is very important and I wanted to make sure you had a second chance to get it right."

Senior chuckled and opened up the box. "This is nice. When you are thinking about doing it?"

"Maybe Christmas."

Senior nodded. "You've proven yourself worthy to take care of her so I have no issues with you having her hand. I haven't seen her this happy in years."

They shook hands and Senior looked in his eyes. "Answer this though...how bad of a beating did you put on Malcolm?"

Indie smirked. "He's not a problem anymore."

CHAPTER TWENTY-TWO

*a*jai A couple months had passed and everything was starting to come full circle. Ricky had been busy getting his storefront together and assisting Indie with whatever other business moves they were making. Taj had been flying back into town every weekend and found a building to start up another branch of her company. And Ajai would be a licensed cosmetologist by the end of the night.

Standing in the full-length mirror, she admired the tiny pudge that poked out through her mustard colored dress. Ajai rubbed the tiny baby bump and smiled at her reflection.

"You look good girl," Ricky complimented walking into the room with Bleu darting around him. "Would you slow down boy?"

"No!" Bleu shouted at the top of his lungs before wrapping himself around Ajai's legs.

Shaking her head and softly laughing at him, Ajai bent over and picked him up. "Thank you. We're going to have two brats running around here. You ready?"

Ricky smiled proudly. "Born ready. If I can't do anything, I can make some pretty babies."

Ajai rolled her eyes and held Bleu close. She wasn't going to argue with him at all. He was right. Bleu looked like every bit of Ricky from his black curly hair to his golden-brown skin. Ajai got lost in Bleu's eyes the same way she got lost in Ricky's. That's what pulled her in the first time she saw Ricky. Ever since then she hadn't been able to turn away.

"You got that," Ajai chuckled. "Are you ready to go? Is everyone going to be on time?"

"Yeah, I talked to Indie before I walked in here. Him and Taj are going to be headed over in a few."

"What about your mom and Senior? They're late to everything."

"Babe, don't worry about anything or anyone else. You are the only one that matters today okay?" Ricky stepped toward her and kissed her lips. "I'm proud of you. You looking good, makin' me look good."

Ajai snorted in laughter and kissed Ricky again before Bleu pushed him away from her. "I've always made you look good."

"You're right about that," Ricky said before tickling Bleu. "Don't be pushing me back boy. That's my momma."

"No, daddy. That's my momma." Bleu finalized with Ajai's signature scowl and folded arms. "No kiss my momma."

"Aight bet," Ricky nodded his head. "Wait until you go to sleep. I'm going to be all over your momma."

"Don't tell him that," Ajai laughed as she plopped down on the bed. "So, are we telling everyone tonight?"

"It's your call, babe. I'm cool on whatever you want to do," Ricky assured her. "We've been keeping it to ourselves since Thanksgiving dinner."

"If I don't tell Taj soon, she's going to tear me a new one for not saying anything about it when I found out."

Ricky snickered. "You're right. We should probably say something at dinner."

He grabbed her shoes off the bench at the end of the bed and slipped them on her feet. "Let's go graduate."

Ajai felt a sense of pride and joy that she'd been searching for years to feel. She did it. She got nudged into stepping into her future and did it. Invincible was the feeling she had, the feeling of being superwoman. After years of breaking down Ricky's product, moving it for him when he had heat on him, they finally made it out.

She picked up her hand from her lap and placed it on Ricky's leg. Ricky shifted his eyes over to her and smiled at her affectionately. "You good, mama?"

"Yeah," she softly hummed. "I am good."

The graduation went by quickly and Taj, Indie and Diane rushed out ahead of her and Ricky without so much as a congratulations.

Ricky snickered at the pensive look on her face as they rode to her celebratory dinner. "So, no one is going to tell me congratulations?"

Ajai huffed and folded her arms over her chest and huffed like a toddler.

"You look like Bleu. That's where he be getting that shit from," Ricky rumbled with laughter. "Cool out, maybe something came up."

"It better be something good because I'm hungry and we are supposed to be doing this together."

Ricky tried not to give away the surprise. Instead of replying he continued toward her hair studio where Indie and Taj were putting the final touches on her gift.

"I forgot how needy you get when you're knocked up. Remind me to stay off of you," Ricky teased making her smack her lips and roll her eyes. "Don't give me that stank face girl."

"I wish you would get off me," Ajai muttered with her lip poked out as Ricky pulled into the complex parking lot. "I know good and well we aren't here so you can work."

Ricky chuckled and parked his car behind Indie's. "Come on."

He grabbed Bleu out the backseat and started into the building, leaving Ajai behind to wrestle with her seat belt, climb out the car, slam it shut and storm into the building behind him. She was so irritated that she couldn't enjoy the beauty of the building. Ajai followed Ricky into the room in the back and the lights turned on and everyone shouted, "Surprise!"

Tears puddled in her eyes and she laughed at herself for being so upset. "I should bust everybody's windows out! Had me thinking that y'all didn't care about me."

Taj beamed and wrapped Ajai in her arms. "Congratulations, I am so proud of you. You should probably go apologize to Ricky for acting up."

Ajai pulled away and looked around. "Wait a minute. Ricky what is this?"

Ricky stood in the crowd next to Indie and Joey. "Your hair studio. Congratulations."

"Don't worry about your rent either, this is all you," Indie added.

Already emotional she couldn't help but cry and thank everyone for investing into her dream and showing up for her. After her tears subsided and everyone was eating and enjoying themselves, she stood up and cleared her throat.

"Alright listen and look at me," she started with a giant smile plastered over her face. "Thank you all for coming and doing this for me. I appreciate it. In light of all the good vibes of today, Ricky and I have a gift we want to share with you...we're expecting baby number two!"

An uproar of noise reverberated off the walls and love flowed through the room. This was what it was all about. Love and family and she finally had it all.

Taj stood by her and hooked her arm in hers. "If it's a girl you should definitely name her after her favorite aunt you know since I missed out on this the first time around."

"You're going to have my child spoiled," Ajai crooned.

"I am."

CHRISTMAS EVE

CHAPTER TWENTY-THREE

*T*aj "I had no clue I was going to be entering Christmas Eve hell," Ricky muttered to himself while Taj stood a few feet away with her hands on her hips and a focused look on her face.

"You've been over here for a day," Joey spoke up. "She's been at this for weeks."

"The house looks like we walked into a Hallmark Christmas movie," Ricky huffed.

While Joey and Ricky went back and forth with their banter, Indie stood on the ladder to secure the angel Taj dug out of Senior's storage. It was the angel her mother adored and made Senior place on the tree every year on Christmas eve. The top of the tree was bare until Christmas Eve. Taj didn't understand why her mother wanted it to happen that way but it was a tradition that she wanted to keep. Especially now that she was permanently back in L.A. and her and Indie were settling into their lives together.

"She's not straight," Taj replied with a sigh looking up at

Indie try to put the angel on top of the tree just right. "Move her a little to the left, babe."

"Nah," Joey spoke up. "That's still not straight."

Taj cut her eyes over at Joey. He clammed up and took a step away. "Does it really matter if the angel is straight or not?"

"Do it really matter if I set you on fire or not?" Taj shot back with a cut of the eye.

Indie straightened the angel and climbed down the ladder. "JoJo leave her alone. Christmas is her holiday and what Baby wants she gets. Plus, I'd rather her have her way then be stomping around here like Ajai."

"How did I get in this?" Ajai questioned from the couch with a plate of cookies that her and Bleu were devouring.

Indie shrugged his shoulders and said, "You just looked like an easy target."

Ajai mouthed kiss my ass and went back to eating her cookies.

"When is Maria getting here?" Indie asked. The mention of Maria's name made Joey's head snap around.

"Maria was that fine ass girl I met a few weeks ago at your place?" he questioned with a brow raised. "Talkin' about she had a man?"

Taj laughed. "Yes Jojo."

"Hmm," he smirked. "What else you need hung Baby? Some mistletoe?"

"I swear," Ricky started up plopping on the couch. "You're never going to get off probation. You can't keep your hands to yourself."

Taj shook her head and rolled her eyes remembering how persistent Joey was with Maria only for her to repeat consistently that she was taken. Joey didn't care though, when he saw something he liked he went after it like a dog to a bone. What he didn't know was that Taj was going to make sure that he had someone in his league to shoot his shot at.

"You sound like a hater," Joey grunted.

Taj zipped past Joey and Ricky and went to make sure the guest rooms were ready. She'd been running around with her head cut on a swivel all day and she hadn't even noticed that she'd barely spoke to or touched Indie outside of telling him where to place the decorations. She had truly channeled her mother to make sure that everything for the holidays was perfect. Taj hadn't celebrated any holiday in years. Every year that passed by she found herself sending Senior a gift and escaping away somewhere where she didn't have to think about not having Bubba or her mother.

Fluffing the pillows and running her hands over the comforter set she heard Indie clear his throat. She looked over her shoulder at him leaning in the doorway with his arms crossed over his chest. "It's a damn shame that I have to chase you around the house so you can give ya nigga a kiss. You been running around all day."

Taj's hiked shoulders dropped realizing that she'd been running around since her feet hit the floor this morning. "I'm sorry. I checked out for a minute."

"I need you to check back in. Everything looks amazing, everything will be fine tomorrow. I need you to stop and breathe. We're supposed to be enjoying each other and relaxing," Indie spoke to her softly and closed the gap between them. The mellowness of his voice seemed to calm her enough to make her tense shoulders relax all the way and her arms to lock around his waist when he was close enough. "Our first Christmas together, I just want to be on chill. We'll have a full house from now until tomorrow night so let's enjoy it."

Taj lightly bit her lip and nodded her head. "Okay."

He craned his neck down to kiss her. Their lips molded

against one another and the heat started rising in the room. Taj was tempted to kick the door shut and take him down before the guests arrived but the chime of the doorbell put a halt to her hands roaming down to the bulge in his gray sweatpants.

"Fuck," Indie groaned. "You owe me."

"I got you. You should probably put on some actual pants because these are telling on you." With one last quick kiss to his caramel lips, Taj hurried to the door before Joey got it.

She was too late. Joey pulled the door open looked past Maria who was standing with her boyfriend to Mackenzie standing on the other side of Maria.

"Got damn," Joey muttered to himself staring at Mackenzie with his mouth open.

Taj's plan had already seemed to be playing out well. Mackenzie tucked her hair behind her ear and ran her eyes over him. "You should close your mouth before something flies in it."

Mackenzie's quip made Joey grunt and his lips turned up into a smile. Before Joey could say something in rebuttal, Taj nudged him out the way and hugged the three of them. "Come in."

"Taj this is gorgeous," Maria gasped admiring the openness of the one-story beach house that was drenched in Christmas decorations. "And it smells like Christmas cookies."

Taj shrugged her shoulders and smiled.

Ricky shouted, "It's an explosion of Hallmark and Taj all in one! Fake snow and shit."

"I really would like for his hatin' ass to shut up," Taj responded brining her guest into the house. "Let me show you to your rooms."

Of course, Joey wasn't too far behind with his persistence. Indie cut the corner and motioned him over. The rumble of Indie's laughter made Taj's smile brighten up the house more than it already was. In turn it made Maria smile.

"Ay what's good Indie?" Indie came over after talking some sense into Joey and greeted Maria's boyfriend with a brotherly hug.

"It's all good, Tristan."

Maria's boyfriend exchanged. "Thanks for having us."

"Any family of Taj is family of mine," Indie replied looking over at Maria and Mackenzie. "Y'all got to excuse my brother. We don't let him out too often."

"Hey Indie," Maria greeted with a laugh. "I warned her on the flight down here that Joey was...passionate."

"I'm a whole lot, baby," Joey commented from the end of the hall.

Taj caught the flushness in Mackenzie's face and smirked to herself. "He's going to be like this all weekend so sorry in advance."

"I'm used to it Mackenzie..." Maria trailed off looking at her sister blush, unable to keep her eyes off of Joey. "Never mind she's going to be fine."

Indie and Tristian broke away with the bags. Maria hooked her arm in Taj's and pulled her away leaving Joey and Mackenzie to have a normal conversation.

"Ajai," Taj's voice rang out in a song. "Maria is here!"

Ajai jumped off the couch and rushed around the guys to throw her arms around her neck. Maria hugged her tight and Taj stood off at the side with a smile on her face. She couldn't ask for a better gift. Her best friends were laughing and embracing each other. This Christmas was going to be one of the best she'd had in ears.

As the day went on Joey made sure to give Mackenzie all of his attention and no one protested it. Joey had a track record of chasing women with no real goal with his overzealous approach but Mackenzie's apparent attraction to him made him calm down a bit.

Senior and Maggie finally showed up along with Diane and Mary. Everyone was getting along and the mood was merry. Taj stood off in the corner with a glass of champagne watching everyone with a smile on her face. She was so happy she couldn't even put it into words.

Feeling Indie's arms engulf her body, she hummed and let her body melt into his. His lips brushed her ear making a shiver run down her spine. Taj loved Indie's touch and whenever she got it, she reacted the same way.

"All your hard work paid off. Everyone is enjoying themselves." She could feel him smile against her ear.

"Thank you, now I can relax." She let her shoulders drop and her head rested on his chest.

Indie chuckled lightly and kissed her exposed skin on her shoulder. "Yeah, but let's do this gift exchange before everyone gets drunk and we can't do shit with them."

"You're right," she hummed looking around the room.

"Aight, y'all. Let's get this gift exchange out the way so we can get drunk and forget everything by brunch tomorrow," Indie announced. Removing his arm from around Taj's waist, he smacked her ass and broke away completely. "Go sit down."

"Let me help."

"Baby, go sit your pretty ass down."

Taj huffed and went to sit down in the armchair. They agreed not to get each other gifts but of course she didn't listen to Indie's suggestion. She smirked smugly to herself when he pulled his gift from under the tree. Indie flashed a look at her and shook his head.

"You don't listen, Baby," he mumbled walking around everyone to kiss her face. "Thank you."

"You're welcome," she hummed watching him kneel down in front of her. Paying it very little mind she sat up hoping he'd opened his gift. "Open it."

"Baby," he chuckled lightly. Obliging her request, Indie opened her gift and smirked at the Swiss timepiece. "Why don't you listen?"

"You can't be a businessman without a good watch," she responded with a shrug.

"Oh yeah?" He chortled and placed the box on the end table beside her chair. "I love you. You know that?"

"I know that," she quickly said in matter of fact tone. "I love you too."

"I know you do. You've shown that time and time again. You held me down, you prayed for me and over me. You've given so much of yourself selflessly and didn't care if you never got it back because you knew...you felt that shit. I've made myself very clear when I said that I will not leave you again, but I want to make sure you know that..."

"Indigoooo," Taj drug out watching him dig into his sweats to retrieve the ring box. "What are you doing?"

"About to lock you down for life because I'm not about to go into the new year without you as my wife. Listen, since the day I met you, my goal has been to make you as comfortable as possible so that you're free to be yourself around me. To give you a sense of security that no one else matters and to give protection. I want to do that forever. So, what do you say? You marryin' a nigga or what?" Indie asked opening the ring box and watching as her eyes watered and lit up at the same time.

Taj forgot about them having a house full of people. She threw her arms around his neck and kissed his lips with passion. Indie forgot about the guests they had too when he engaged her.

"You horny ass niggas ain't alone!" Ricky shouted bringing them back to reality. "Give her the ring so we can roll up and celebrate!"

Taj giggled against Indie's lips as he peeked over to make

sure he was sliding the ring on her tattooed finger. "Just wait until later."

"I'm waiting on forever." Indie stood to his feet and pulled Taj up along with him. The ring was the least of her concerns. She just wanted to stand in his arms and inhale his scent before they were pulled away from each other. Indie nuzzled his face into her curls and held her securely.

Finally, they broke away from each other and Taj stuck her hand out and grinned. Maria and Ajai quickly shuffled over to examine Indie's stop sign for any man approaching her.

"That's how you do it!" Joey embraced his brother. "I'm proud of you."

"Thanks bro." Indie grinned.

Ricky placed his hand on his shoulder and handed him a shot of tequila. "We're proud of you, nigga. On hood."

The guys migrated outside to light and pour up and the girls huddled up around the food and wine to celebrate everything that happened through the year and everything that was soon to come.

After hours of celebrating, dancing, and games everyone finally broke off to their rooms to get sleep in preparation for the next day.

Indie and Taj slipped out during the last game to enjoy each other. They didn't mind putting on a show, but they didn't want to scare anyone.

Taj laid on her stomach next to Indie who laid on his side with his hands in her hair. "I don't want to wait long to get married."

"Whatever you want you go it."

"Like six months, tops."

Indie yawned and closed his eyes. "Just tell me where to show up. It's your show."

CHAPTER TWENTY-FOUR

*I*ndie
      Six months flew by and between Taj's wedding planning, opening up her office there and establishing her clients, Indie was having a hell of a time catching up with her. But tomorrow all of her running around would come to a stop for a week or two and he would have her to himself.

Since Taj had been kidnapped by Ajai and Maria tonight, Ricky made plans to show Indie a good time. They were in Crenshaw riding down the street with the windows down and the music playing like it was back in the day and they were young niggas with nothing to lose.

Indie sat on the passenger side blowing smoke from his nostrils and bopping his head to the music playing. The more they rode around the more his mind flashed back on everything that he went through in these streets. Then he looked around at his brothers and smirked to himself.

"Nigga," Indie started over the music as Ricky pulled into the same parking lot at the beach where his epiphany took place. "You know we were some wild ass niggas."

Ricky parked the car and killed the engine and hopped out of the car. "Nigga, you ain't lying. Out here shooting niggas for nothing at all."

"I just need to go on record and say you started that shit. Had me out here firing back with no fuckin' issue." Indie chuckled hopping out the car and relighting his blunt. "Shooting niggas, fighting over corners, serving sets. If you think about all of that, we weren't supposed to make it out. We should've been in the grave."

Joey nodded his head and leaned his back against the trunk of the car. "We made it. That shit is heavy. Like it makes you really think about the shit we doin' now. Y'all niggas out here about to get married with kids. This is big shit. Y'all are the epitome of *nigga we made it*. I'm for real proud of y'all. I got to catch up.

"How's things going with Mackenzie?" Indie asked looking at his brother. Joey's face beamed with the mention of her name making Indie and Ricky nudge each other back and forth and chuckle. "That good huh? You got you a little something something?"

"She's something special," Joey replied with a smile.

"It's written all over your face. And you not acting like a fuckin' creep. That's how I know you feelin' her. Remember all the game I taught you," Indie returned opening a bottle of Crown Royal.

"I will. What you think I've been using to get me this far? All that free game ain't going to waste. How are you feeling though?" Joey questioned.

"Who me? Nigga I'm smooth. I'm ready though. She's been running around getting everything situated. I'm ready to have her to myself."

Joey scoffed at Indie's comment. "You're selfish you know that. Had you just shared before you wouldn't be standing here with that stupid grin on your face. Baby would have been mine but that's cool. You go ahead and marry her and make her happy. Y'all deserve that much."

"I swear you're annoyin'," Ricky chuckled.

"Hell yeah he is." Indie laughed taking a swig from the bottle and handing it over to Ricky. "But for real though. This shit feels amazing to be where we're standing looking back at all the shit we did and where we are. Tomorrow isn't just my wedding, it's our celebration of life."

"Bet," Ricky nodded handing the body to Joey and lighting up a blunt of his own. "I'm going to say this and be done cause a nigga is going to get emotional as fuck. I love y'all niggas like on everything. I lost my brother to the streets and for a while I struggled with finding my footing and maneuvering through my anger, but you stayed solid even when I was out here running around like I knew it all. You showed me who you were time and time again and you showed up. When I say I am happy for you and Taj I mean that with every ounce of my heart. That's a love that withstood the test of time and is all yours man. Keep taking care of her and she'll hold you down forever."

Indie embraced Ricky. "You my brother, nigga. I love you for real."

"Always bro."

CHAPTER TWENTY-FIVE

Taj "Come on Taj," Taj murmured to herself and wiped the tears from her eyes. "Get it together."

She decided not to go downstairs to dinner with Mary, Diane, Maggie, Ajai and Maria. Taj woke up with tears falling out her eyes. Five years without her brother and she didn't want today to be filled with sad memories of him. She wanted it to be full of joy and love, but she couldn't get him off of her mind.

"Bubba," she cried silently into the covers. "Come on." The hotel room was still dark although it was close to eleven in the morning. "I miss you but I'm okay."

She figured talking through her emotions would help her feel better and make her get up and ready to start the preparation for tonight. "I'm happy...I listened to everything you told me. I have a thriving business. And if you were here you would tell me to stop crying and get up."

Taj sat up in the bed and wiped her face. "It's all for you Bubba. Thank you for everything."

After a few quiet moments of getting herself together, she pushed herself out the bed and shuffled over to the windows to pull the curtains open and then the balcony. She welcomed the view of the Santa Monica and breeze to grace her flesh. Once her nerves were officially calm, she texted Maria and asked her to bring some food for her before the day got hectic.

The counter on her home screen counted down the hours and minutes until her and Indie stood at the small altar and vowed their love for each other. From the balcony, she sauntered into the bathroom and got ready for her day.

When everyone returned back to the suite they were getting ready in, Taj was sitting on the couch with her legs tucked under her butt with her wet hair dripping on her robe. "Look who's up," Maggie's voice rang out into the room making Taj look up from her computer screen.

"I know you better not be working?" Maria sounded off behind Maggie. "I told you I took care of both locations already. Could you relax and enjoy today?"

Taj groaned and closed her laptop before dropping her head back.

Diane walked in with Mary and looked at Taj. "Why are you nervous? Nothing is changing, you two are just putting your union on paper. We are not pouting today."

The cork of champagne popping indicated the end of Diane's statement. "We are going to party and drink and have a great time. That's all that matters."

That's all that Taj needed to hear to completely take her out of her funk. Champagne was flowing, Mary was dancing around the room and Maria was sure not to miss a minute of any of this footage.

While Ajai started blowing Taj's hair out, Maria slipped out the room to meet Indie in the hall. Taj could see him out the corner of her eye as he tried to hide behind the door.

"You are so nosey," Ajai hummed drawing Taj's attention back. "It's killing you not to see him huh?"

Taj looked back in the mirror she was sitting in front of and nodded. "You have no idea. A few more hours though."

"For Indie to be who he is to everyone he is putty when it comes to you. You need to write a book on how you got him to trust you and fall the way he did," Ajai teased.

"I can't give away my secrets." Taj chuckled seeing Maria walk back in out the corner of her eye.

Maria closed the door with a smile on her face and strolled over to Taj. "I have a gift and a message for you from your husband."

"Oh, that sounded so good can you say it again?" Taj requested.

"From your husband," Maria repeated with a giggle. "He wanted you to have this before you got your makeup done and he said to be sure you wore it down the aisle."

Maria placed the long jewelry box in Taj's hand. "Indie wanted to make sure that you felt like today was a day of new beginnings. He said he understands and feels how important it is for you to have a piece of Bubba here with you today. He also said he loves you and can't wait to get his hands on you."

Taj opened the bow and looked down at the diamond chain with Bubba's name encrusted on the charm in diamonds. Her eyes fluttered with tears. "That man. I swear."

Taking it out the box, she ran her fingers over it and grinned. "I'm not crying anymore," Taj protested placing the necklace back in the box.

After her hair and make was done and the room swarmed with photographers to capture the beauty of this day, she was zipped into her silk gown and Maria clasped the necklace around her neck.

Senior's voice rumbled from the living room of the suite. "Is she ready?"

"Yeah," Taj spoke up. "Come in."

Senior didn't waste any time walking into the room to lay his eyes on his daughter. His voice got caught in this throat when he laid eyes on her. Taj could see that Senior was about to have a moment and she wanted to share it with him privately.

"Can y'all give us a minute?" she asked looking back at the girls nod their heads, walk out and close the door behind them. "You look good, Daddy."

Taj trailed her eyes over his blue suit and adored how well it looked on him. His salt and pepper hair was cut into a low fade and his goatee was edged up. "You look like one of those seasoned old men out of GQ."

Senior chuckled before saying, "Girl I look like a player. Feel like one too."

"Don't let Maggie hear that."

"Ah, she knows what she has and she likes it too. You look like your mother," he spoke proudly letting a few tears run down his face. "So beautiful, so happy. She's smiling down and so is Bubba."

"I know, I can feel it. Thank you for being here."

"I wouldn't miss this day for the world, Baby. I know I have been the hardest person to love and to get along with, but I thank you for not counting me out," Senior shared wrapping his hand around hers. "I am so proud of everything you have done and the woman you have become. I never saw this day happening, but I want you to know that this is another lap in your race. Don't let the little things that come up turn into big things that make you stop. Love with all your heart and dance like nobody's watching. I love you."

"I love you, Daddy," Taj hugged him and stood on her tip toes to kiss his cheek. "It's almost time."

"Before I walk you down the aisle, I want you to have this." Senior dug into his pocket and pulled out his late wife's sapphire bracelet. "She always talked about keeping this so you could wear it on your wedding day. I made sure to keep it close. This is yours now."

Clasping it around her wrist, Senior brought Taj's knuckles to his lips. "I'll be waiting outside on you."

"I'll be out in a minute."

Just as Senior stepped out the door the girls came flooding back in to finish getting Taj ready. She lost track of the time it took to get out of the room and down to the area set up by the pools. The heat of the day was overtaken by the breeze from the ocean. The music played softly while the guests waited for her to drift down the aisle.

As she peeked around the corner, she could see the shades of flowers from white to indigo line the aisle and the rest on the cocktail tables ten feet away from the ceremony site. While Taj waited for the song to switch over to her song, she peeped at Indie shifting in his stance and looking up at the sky. She rubbed her lips together and squeezed Senior's hand.

"Are you ready?" he whispered in her ear.

Taj nodded her head hearing the song switch and ring out through the courtyard. "I'm ready."

Taking a step out into the open, Taj's eyes automatically locked with Indie's. Seeing his face turn red and his nostrils flare in order to combat the emotion begging to be freed. It felt like an eternity before she reached the altar and promptly gave her hands over to Indie's custody. But not before she reached up and wiped the tear from his cheek.

Mouthing, you look good, forced him to smile through his unspeakable joy toward her.

While the officiant began the ceremony while Taj and Indie shared looks, smiles and soft laughs all the way up until the officiant said, "The couple has decided to write their own vows."

Taj squeezed his hand as she took a deep inhale and braced for Indie's words to grace her ear. He cleared his throat and looked deep into her eyes like no one else showed up to witness this day but the two of them. "I'm not sure if you know this. But judging how well you know me you might. Taj Ali...you saved my life. You stepped into my world with a calming power I never came in contact with before. You were so soft and loving and you were always too good to be true. There were plenty of days that I wondered if I were dreaming or was holding you and being able to submerge myself in you really real. When you were pulled from me, I knew. I knew that this indeed was real and no matter how long it took I had to get it back. Tomorrow we're going to wake up husband and wife and that's going to push me to love you more, trust you more, and protect you more than I already do. I've never been prouder than I am right now to look at you and to say Thank God we made it. Thank God for blessing me with a woman that carried my spirit in her heart. Although I lost it, I knew where to find it. I vow to love you more each day and to remember where we came from and look at where we are going. Taj Ali Sims, you are my light, you are my world and you have my heart forever...on hood!"

"On hood!" Joey and Ricky chimed in throwing up the set before Taj could continue with her vows.

"So, Indigo Sims...I didn't know what it was like to love until you made me do it. In all seriousness it was hard not to. I would try to stop loving you, but my heart yearned for you more. I knew then that you were my home. The place where my mind found rest. A place that God set up camp so my soul could be still. It has been my highest honor to love you. My highest honor to have you. My highest honor to feel you. You are my lover, my best friend, my soul mate, my reason and protector. I will forever love you without reservation. I will continue to house your spirit and nurture it so that we can grow together. I am thankful that my prayers were heard, and that God revealed Himself. Today is another day, another lap, another chance and I vow to carry that gratitude until we are no more. You are where all my dreams live, and you have made it easy to entrust you with me. To most people you're hard and you are a fearless leader but to me, you're soft, and your heart is kind, and your spirit is good. To me, you're king and you've made me comfortable enough to stand by you and be queen. For that I'm indebted."

The officiant motioned Ricky for the rings. Indie didn't wait for her to announce him and Taj as husband and wife. He grabbed her by the waist and locked lips with her and the guests cheered, wiped tears and applauded.

"I now pronounce you, Mr. and Mrs. Indigo Sims!"

INDIGO PULLED Taj out of the reception so he could have her to himself on the terrace from a few minutes. Taj rested her head on his chest loving the sound of his heart pounding against it. She inhaled his scent while he tightened his arms around her.

"Before tonight gets really wild, I just wanted you to know that you never have to worry about anything," he muttered. "I got you."

Taj lifted her head up and looked at him. "I know. And I want you to know the same. I got you. Everything you fear, everything you tuck away, everything you love, and everything you find peace in is safe with me."

"You better stop talking to me like that before I give these people a damn show."

Taj threw her head back in laughter. "They won't be able to handle it babe."

"I know they won't so stop talkin' that shit to me. You know what it does to me."

"And you know what you do to me."

Indie smirked and craned his neck to kiss his petite bride before Senior grumbled and drew their attention to him. "I'll let y'all finish. I wanted to tell you both that I am proud of you. Indie be soft with her and Taj you do the same. This commitment you two made today won't be easy. You're not going to like each other at points but remember the reason why. Remember what bonded you two in the first place. Taj, it wasn't the loss of Bubba that put you here. It was the promise of a new beginning. Don't forget that...aight?"

Senior kissed Taj's forehead and then embraced Indie. "Thank you, cuh."

"Cuh?" Taj questioned pinning her brows together. "Daddy is there something you failed to tell me?"

"You don't have to know everything little lady." Senior smirked. "Just know that this was destined to happen no matter how hard I fought it. The party is about to start."

Taj looked up at Indie. "You knew."

"Of course, I knew. But that's not important."

"Then what is?" Taj questioned as Indie bit his lip.

He leaned down to her and grunted in her ear. "You backing that ass up on Zaddy."

EPILOGUE

$\mathcal{O}$ne Year Later

Everyone was gathered in the private room of the restaurant that Joey opened a few months back. They were celebrating Indie's birthday with all his favorites, stories, and Indie's line of marijuana. Joey was sure to put them all the way in the back of the building and open up the doors to the patio so the other guests outside the dining area wouldn't have anything to complain about.

In the last year, Ricky started his retail store, Ajai opened another salon and UCLA partnered with Indie to sponsor the STEM program. Everything that they wanted they obtained and now their dreams were getting bigger.

Pulling up to the valet of the restaurant, Indie hopped out and handed the valet the keys out his pocket. He traveled around the car to help Taj out the car. He helped her out and shut the door. "You were right, I probably should've driven the other car," he snickered lowly hearing Taj groan and try to straighten out her back with her huge belly.

"I'm happy you realize that...now," Taj moaned and rubbed her belly. I'm not getting back in there after tonight."

"You're probably going to have to drive home too," he stated.

Taj groaned again and placed her hand on her back before wobbling into the restaurant. "You know if I weren't pregnant with twins I would be happy to drive that. I have to figure out how to get my ass back in that thing."

Indie couldn't help but laugh. "Your ass is looking great though."

"Why thank you baby, hopefully I can keep it," Taj hummed and tried to straighten up her walk while she wobbled through the restaurant and into the private room.

Indie laughed. "Just wobble, Baby. It's cool. That's all me."

They entered the private dining room and greeted their guests. As dinner went on everyone was sure to tell their favorite story of Indie.

"I didn't get to meet Indie until a year ago," Maria spoke up "But when I did, I knew that there was something special about him. He has this energy about him that you can't help but to love him and I think that I speak for all of us when I say it is a gift to know him and have been welcomed into his world with open arms. Happy birthday young king."

"On hood." Indie chuckled feeling the champagne running through his system. He looked over at Taj. "You know you got to top all of them."

"I don't have to. I'm married to you that's my toast," Taj joked standing to her feet. "So, babe, the last year of your life has been so much fun for you."

She pointed to her belly. "Clearly."

"Looks like it's been fun for you too." Indie laughed. "What you talkin' about? We about to have some more fun tonight."

Taj shook her head and rolled her eyes. "Anyways. What I

love about you are the same things people have been saying all night. Your love is so big. Your heart is so big. And your energy is contagious. You stand for something and you lead the way. And when it comes to me you make sure I'm supported even if it takes time for you. My brother used to say, Baby live your life and grow and reach your heights. So Indigo, live your life baby, grow and reach all the heights you want. You have me and a whole gang of niggas who will stand behind you and push you and follow you without question. And that's on hood!"

"On hood!" Indie cheered standing up to throw his arm over Taj's shoulder and pull her into him as he held his drink up. "To love, to life, to living everyday like tomorrow ain't promised. To the marathon."

"To the marathon."

THE END

DJ KHALED FEATURING NIPSEY HUSSLE & JOHN LEGEND: HIGHER

Lookin' back at my life made my heart race
Dance with the devil and test all faith
I was thinkin' chess moves, but it was God's grace
You keep takin' me higher and higher
Don't you know that the devil is a liar
I know they'd rather see me down with my soul in the fire
But we keep going higher, higher

After everything I've even set out in life to do, this had been one of the most difficult. One of the most rewarding. One of the most fulfilling things I'd ever done. Not because it was something trendy to do in the moment of grief. But because for so much he gave; this was the least I could give back. I spent countless hours listening to his voice on a loop so I could do this project justice.

And it was dreamt, it was felt, it was completed.

There are very few people in this lifetime who had the reach and the power that Ermias did. A prophet among men, a light for those in the darkest of places, and a constant beckon of hope.

This is my personal dedication - my tribute.

We will never forget your message nor anything Nipsey Hussle stood for because he passed the torch on to us. It is my personal mission to carry out the Marathon. To use my platform to inspire and encourage the voiceless. To show everyone that love in whatever form it is given is worthy of having. That no matter what route you took to get to your finish line that it's worthy of a victory lap and a celebration.

Whatever mission you are on in life is worth your all. It will not be easy. No gift given by God will ever be easy to have. Protect your light and your energy. You will feel every emotion. You will win and you will lose. But always remember that the race is up to you. The win is up to you. Every reaction to every outcome is up to you. Run your lap. Win your race, and after you've won,

run your victory lap. Your work will talk for you and your faith-
fulness will open doors that pride could never open.
With love,
A.P.
TMC
Rest in Paradise Ermias "Nipsey Hussle" Asghedom.

ALSO BY AUBREÉ PYNN

LOVE WILL FOREVER BE CONSISTENT

Thank you for reading! Make sure you check out my catalog:

Color Me, You

SumWhereOvaRainbows: A Collection of Poetry

Connect with me on my social media:

IG: @aubreepynn

TWITTER: @aubreepynn

Facebook: Aubreé Pynn

Check out my website:

Aubreepynnwrites.wordpress.com

A million words, in a million books, is never thank you enough for your support.

CPSIA information can be obtained
at www.ICGtesting.com
Printed in the USA
LVHW041934211019
634862LV00004B/896/P